CITY MUSE

CITY MUSE

THE MUSE SERIES
BOOK 1

PRU WARREN

QUI
LEGIT
REGIT
PRESS
She who reads, rules

This is a work of fiction. Any references to historical events, real people, or real locales are used fictitiously. Other names, characters, places, and incidents are products of the author's imagination, and any resemblance to actual events or locales or persons, living or dead, is entirely coincidental.

Cover design by The Killion Group

Published by Qui Legit Regit Press
Alexandria, Virginia

ISBN 979-8-9883359-7-9

Discover other titles by Pru Warren at https://www.pruwarren.com/

092923wch

Created with Vellum

CONTENTS

1. Definitely Not My Best	1
2. Breaking the Camel's Back	6
3. Shattering the Silence	11
4. Gabbing with My Girls	21
5. Late-Night Conversations	28
6. The Daily Grind	36
7. Have Kayak, Will Travel	46
8. All-Class Field Trip	53
9. Bart in the Back Seat	64
10. Coffeehouse Concert	70
11. November Snows	82
12. In the Blizzard	92
13. Social Noshing	102
14. Weathering the Chill	116
15. Featherbed Lane	128
16. Truths	145
17. Numbness Is Easy	153
18. Ignoring Despair	159
19. The Talent Show	171
20. Second Act	183
Want to read Cleo's Story?	197
Bliss & Giggles	199
About the Author	201
Also by Pru Warren	203

1

DEFINITELY NOT MY BEST

CALLIE

I wish to plead guilty. I was unpardonably rude when I first met my daughter's high school biology teacher, but there were extenuating circumstances. You should have seen his posterior.

He had his back to the classroom door, all defenseless in the silence of a school after the closing bell and not expecting to be verbally assaulted. I came around the corner, saw him, and was so worked up over the way my day had gone that I stupidly spoke before I could edit myself.

"Jesus God, you don't wear those pants in front of your *students*, do you?"

He whirled, his hands going to one of the finest behinds I'd ever seen to check for rips or tears. He needn't have done it. He was technically decent. It's just that he was wearing a faded pair of jeans that clung lovingly to those perfect buttocks.

I was immediately flustered. My fault, of course. But when confronted with social anxiety, my reaction has always been to come out swinging. That reaction has made me a vicious, successful lawyer, but it would definitely work against me in building the kind of parent-teacher relationship that would benefit my daughter.

"I'm—I'm sorry?" he sputtered.

Damn. The front view of the guy was as attractive as the back. Shaggy, sandy hair framing a strong jaw. Blue eyes that matched the denims. The biology teacher was a looker.

And just like that, I understood what was going on with my daughter.

Leigh had seemed to slip easily into the routine of a new school. The first three weeks of seventh grade at Hamilton Academy had been going great—except that my unnaturally practical, orderly daughter had taken to doodling, sighing, watching old black-and-white movies, and jumping guiltily when startled. I had no idea what was going on with her and hadn't yet uncovered the cause for her insanity.

And here the reason stood, blinking in front of me as if bathed in an invisible spotlight. Angelic choirs all but sang in wreaths around his head. I controlled my wince of discomfort.

Leigh had clearly developed her first crush. On her bio teacher.

My baby was growing up, and I didn't like it.

"The pants," I said. There was no hiding from the reality that my tone was snide. "A little tight, don't you think?"

"Uh," he said, then regrouped. "Are you Mrs. Peacham?"

"I wasn't Mrs. Peacham even when I *was* married to Leigh's father. I'm Callie Lyndon." I thrust out a businesslike hand. That's how women shake hands in the land of corporate law: fast, firm, decisive. It's a don't-screw-with-me handshake, and it's designed to put the other guy at a disadvantage.

It worked.

He shook my hand like he wished he had on safety gloves. "I'm sorry. I'm sure I knew that."

I hid the rippling pain of the still-recent divorce behind an arrogant nod to acknowledge his attempt to appease me. "You wanted to meet with me? I've got about ten minutes before I have to head back to my office. I suggest we get right to it."

He blinked and stammered for a moment, looking at me through a fall of dark blond hair. He probably knew how cute that was, I thought in irritation. "I'm sorry. Can I have a moment?" he said.

To my astonishment, he turned to his desk and fished for paper. I blinked back my surprise while he scribbled something quickly and then spilled out a series of dots across the page. I was about to clear my throat significantly when he held up one finger, silently asking for another moment. I shifted my weight in frustration.

He turned back with a shattering smile. "Thanks so much. Now, let me show you why I asked you to meet with me."

He grabbed a tablet, tapped it, and the school's home screen appeared on the whiteboard at the front of the room. He stood next to me while pulling up the assignments from the biology class.

"Look," he said. "I wanted you to see Leigh's paper on food webs. Did you review it before she turned it in?"

He didn't mean to sound accusing, and in fact, he probably wasn't—but that was what I heard. Leigh and I had moved to New York City just weeks before the start of the school year, and I was running at double speed to get caught up at my new job. Leigh, the most organized, disciplined child anyone would ever meet, had never needed me to review her homework when we lived in Washington, DC. I'd assumed she wouldn't need it in this school either.

But I didn't let a nagging sense of guilt show. *Always answer only the question asked. Volunteer nothing more.* That was my rule. "No," I replied.

"Okay. Here's what she submitted."

The screen at the front of the classroom showed a nicely typed paper, evenly spaced with no obvious typos. I scanned the first few lines. "This looks pretty good. What's the problem?"

He smiled. "It's a little *too* good for seventh grade."

"My daughter is very bright. Perhaps you haven't realized that yet."

"Oh, I have realized that. She's a great student and a sweet kid. But she's not the author of this paper."

A corporate litigator can be pretty intimidating when she wants to be. "What are you implying?"

Instead of answering, he began fiddling with the tablet again, going through a Google search until he pulled up a graduate thesis from 2013. The introduction was different, but it wasn't long before I came to a paragraph that was identical to Leigh's paper. "Goddamn it."

I didn't usually swear; it was too easy to slip up in the courtroom and risk offending juries or judges. But this one flew out of me without a single warning. My control was slipping, and that wouldn't do.

More importantly, how much trouble was my daughter in?

At my core, I didn't think of myself as a tough cookie. But I bet the bio teacher would have disagreed, based on the fierce attitude that slammed like steel doors over my quivering heart like armor.

His eyes had drifted to the paper on his desk. I cleared

my throat to regain his attention. "Have you asked Leigh about this?"

"No. I thought I'd better talk to you about it first."

Thank god. She wasn't on the brink of suspension. I hid my relief and nodded briskly. "I'll take care of this. What are her options?"

He shrugged. "I'll give her two more days. If she wants to turn in an original paper, I'll delete this one. *This* time." He looked down at me, which was unusual; at five-foot-ten, I was tall for a woman. "She only gets one Get Out of Jail Free card, though. Will you tell her?"

"I'll make it clear." I focused on him and held out my hand for another don't-screw-with-me shake. "Thank you for bringing this to me. And Mr. Thetford?" I refused to release his hand, tugging him slightly toward me and thus off-balance. "Don't wear those jeans in front of my daughter again."

He blinked and looked as if he was about to utter a startled laugh. Before he could make that serious mistake, I wheeled around to leave.

Only to see trouble standing in the doorway.

2

BREAKING THE CAMEL'S BACK

CALLIE

"Callie, darlin'!"

Addie Belle McCrillis was hugging the doorjamb as if she were too coy to come fully into the room.

"Bart, honey, can I borrow Callie for a bit?" She smiled her high-wattage smile, pearly teeth gleaming like the promise of absolution.

"We're done," he said. "Nice to meet you, Ms. Lyndon." I was dismissed. He was turning back to the scribbles on his page before I'd even left the room.

Damn it. That did not make for a power exit.

And there stood my new boss's wife. Addie Belle, Atlanta's darling, was the reason Leigh had been accepted into Hamilton Academy. Addie Belle was on the school board and cut a wide swath. Married to the managing partner of one of the biggest corporate law firms in Manhattan, Addie Belle held a position of social prominence that she managed very closely.

My instinctive dislike of her was ungrateful. When Lawrence McCrillis tapped me to work on the AresCorp case and pulled me from the relative obscurity of the DC branch, Addie Belle was the one who'd found the sublet we were living in—and the garage where we could afford to keep the Volvo.

So, there was no logical reason she set my teeth on edge. I supposed it was because she was everything I wasn't: Addie Belle was curvy and girly where I was straight and athletic. She was delicate and feminine where I consciously took the sway out of my walk. She was known for her signature Hermès scarves and the intense care she took of her skin and honey-colored hair to look young at a time when I was wearing clear-glass frames and cutting my dark hair to look as mature as possible.

But I was no fool. I could see the writing on the wall. One word of praise from her to her husband one night over a high-society dinner, and I'd be on the fast track to partner. One moue of disappointment, and I'd be back in DC before the week was out.

So, Addie Belle was an important person in my life.

She drew me into the hall, waggling her fingers over her shoulder at Mr. Thetford. "Toodles, Bart!" She turned to me. "I was so glad to learn you're here, Callie. I'm just in the worst pickle, and you're the girl to pull me out of it!"

Addie Belle looked at me to make sure I was excited to hear her tale. I slipped into sycophantic anticipation without even hating myself for doing it. "Why? What happened?"

She tucked her hand into the crook of my elbow and drew me down the hallway to the main office. Had she intentionally cast me in the male role while she both clung to me and directed me at her will—a classic Powerful Little Woman move?

"You know Delilah Stratford? No? Her Tanner is in

fourth grade here." She leaned in confidingly. "A little problem with self-control, but a bright child, really." She nodded at me significantly, and I fought an irrational burst of scorn. "Well, Lilah's husband has just been made ambassador to Brunei. Isn't that exciting?"

Sounded to me like Tanner's father had made a big political contribution, but more power to him. I hoped Delilah would like lying on a beach all day.

Addie Belle continued her confidences. "Of course, you know Lilah chairs the school's most important fundraiser—the parent-student-teacher talent show in March."

"Of course." I'd never heard of the talent show; we'd been a part of the school for all of three weeks.

"We're desperate for someone else to take it on." She tugged on my elbow, stopping me in the long hall and facing me. She looked at me significantly.

"Oh," I said after too long a pause. "And you want me—"

"Darlin'!" she cooed. "I don't *want* you. I *need* you!" She started us walking again as I absorbed the news. "Simply everyone else with any brains at all is already doing something. You know how important volunteerism is among the parents at Hamilton. I told you about that, didn't I?"

She looked at me with sudden suspicion, and I nodded quickly. "You did. I'm already a driver for the field trip next Tuesday."

"Oh, wonderful," she said. "It's such a fun day. You'll love it. But about the talent show—this year, we're raising money to expand that weather thing on the roof. WeatherNet."

"You mean the Hamilton PrimaryNet? Leigh's all over that program."

"There, you see? You're the right person for the job!"

My daughter had filled me in breathlessly. The PrimaryNet was the brainchild of one of Hamilton's math teachers, who had wanted to use meteorology to make the use of mathematics real. Of course, all the school's math and science teachers were in favor.

And because this was Hamilton and not just any school, they'd gotten involved with the National Oceanic and Atmospheric Administration—NOAA for short—and were now part of a weather forecasting network. The big time. This school had all the bells and whistles.

Addie brought me back to our discussion. "The STEM team wants to bring primary schools across the state into the net, and that's what we're raising money for at the talent show. A worthy cause, isn't it?" She waited for me to nod back at her, perhaps feeling that now that I'd agreed, she'd firmly set her hook. "Now, I know it's a great deal of work, Callie darlin', and you're simply swamped with the Ares-Corp case. I asked Lawrence what he thought of the idea, and he said he thought you could handle it. But it's a lot of work. Is he right? Can you?"

Could I handle it?

Could I tackle a fundraiser at a hopelessly wealthy school full of energy vampires clustering around to draw the life essence from my body for the next half year, while being the point person on a morally suspect legal case that would establish both federal and military law for generations to come?

While also raising a daughter in the aftermath of a shattering divorce and trying to help the woman I regarded as a grandmother, who was determined to remain in a rapidly decaying home?

Addie Belle's smile told the story. I could decline and focus on my career, which would, perversely, be devastating to my career.

Or I could accept and somehow find extra hours in the

day while juggling competing demands on my time, skills, and attention, which would only be devastating to my career if I screwed up in any of the goals laid before me.

So, not a choice at all.

All right, then. Superwoman works best when she works alone.

"I'm yours to command, Addie Belle. Tell me what you want me to do."

"Oh, you utter darlin'!" she squealed in excitement. "Come into the teacher's lounge. Let me lay this out for you."

"Well," I said unhappily. "I guess I've got a few minutes."

"Oh, sure," she said. "I'm sure we can cover most of it in no time."

This would make it hard to maintain moral authority over my maybe-not-skilled-enough team at work. It would be tough to assert dominance over underlings for wasting my time when I then turned around and wasted their time.

I'd figure it out.

3

SHATTERING THE SILENCE

BART

Ever since the Warrior Mommy stomped into my classroom, I'd been hearing a flute.

Not like the school band was practicing in the auditorium. I wasn't hearing a *real* flute. It was an ethereal, pure, perfect flute. It sounded like liquid silver. It was playing a single line over and over—a clear, descending line flattening out at the bottom before arpeggios flipped it up to a high siren call.

It sounded like someone in pain but still reaching out. There was fear and hope in that single line of music. It was the sound of courage against all odds.

Did I sound psychotic? *Bart, do the flutes ever tell you to do bad things?*

No. I wasn't that kind of crazy. For as long as I could remember, I've heard music. I'd written two jingles for local Vermont stores by the time I was fourteen, a national jingle when I was sixteen (if you lived in a farming part of the US, then you'd probably heard that one: "Let it grow, let it show, your Future—Farmers Savings Bank." It's not Shakespeare, but it's catchy.)

And I'd sold a song to a band when I was seventeen that got to the Top 40 on the country charts. I'd thought maybe I could be a musician or songwriter.

At least, I'd hoped that until I stopped hearing music.

I wasn't an idiot. I knew my problem was psychological. I even knew what caused it.

I just didn't know what I wanted to do about it.

See, too many people around me have died.

The same summer that "Alison's Tractor" made it to the charts for the Zac Brown Band, my father was killed in a freak accident. He'd been driving back from delivering milk to the dairy co-op when a trucker on a back road was texting his girlfriend or fishing for a new radio station or some damned thing. We didn't really know what because when the semi plowed into my father's truck, they both went off the bridge and into the Ompompanoosuc. They both died.

So, that was pretty horrible. But I could still hear music after that.

My mom had insisted I go on to college, although she asked me again if I'd switch to the ag school at the University of Vermont instead of studying music. She'd always wanted me to take over the family dairy farm after her. "You'd be the seventh generation of my family on this land," she said pleadingly.

I pointed out that my sister, Alison, was jumping up and down, hand in the air, begging to run the farm, and the seventh generation was waiting to take over. But after Dad died, it got harder to make the argument.

We compromised on dendrology, in the School of Environmental Sciences—the study of trees. She thought I could work for the Forest Service. And I thought that was a pretty good idea . . . although I packed in as many music classes and voice and guitar lessons as I could while at UVM. Even some keyboard and recording study.

Mom's brother, Henry, helped her run the dairy for the two years Ali and I were both at UVM (Alison, of course, couldn't wait to get to the ag school, and she and Mom put their heads together all the time over her new ideas for better farm management). After I graduated, I moved to New York City with my drummer, Bump, to see if we could make a go at being musicians, and Ali fulfilled our mother's dreams by making Cloverleaf Farms the center of her existence. The seventh generation of making land profitable in a determinedly rocky (if utterly beautiful) part of the world.

Things were going great. Bump and I were getting gigs, I was hearing music in every sound, Mom was happy—then Ali was diagnosed with pancreatic cancer.

They didn't know how she got it. The doctor pointed out that if it had been the presence of farming chemicals, other farmers would be getting pancreatic cancer at a higher rate than normal, and they weren't. He said I needed to give up trying to find out why.

Ali died eight horrible months after her diagnosis. Bump canceled all our gigs so I could spend time with her. It was a bad time to step away from the music scene, since we were getting some attention, but for me, it wasn't a choice.

When Ali died, it was a blessing. A kindness. Death came as a friend to a beautiful young woman in grisly, unending pain.

And even then, I could still hear music.

But before I could even draw a breath, Mom sold the farm. She moved into a retirement community in Burlington and wouldn't look me in the eye. She insisted she was fine; she didn't want to be at the farm anymore. But she said it to my ear or my throat or my hairline. She wouldn't look at me.

And that was when I stopped hearing music.

Wait—let me clarify. I could hear music. I just couldn't hear *my* music.

There was no longer any music in the sound of speeding cars on wet pavement. There was no music in a slamming window or an Uber driver yelling at a garbage man who's got the street blocked. There was nothing at all for me in the call of crickets in a field.

And that was okay with me.

If giving up music was the price for the guilt of still being alive after losing my father and my sister and finally, like trying to hold water in your cupped hands, my mother —I figured I deserved it.

For three years, I heard silence. Bump and I still gigged. We played my old songs and covered other people's work, but I was thirty-two now, and that was pretty old to break into the rock world. Still okay for folk or blues, but rock was where the big money was and where my soul used to be, so I pretty much resigned myself to a life in education instead of music.

Numb was easier.

And then—that flute.

For the first time in three years, I heard a melody.

The Warrior Mommy who confronted me was furious that I'd had to stop her long enough to write down that melody; I wouldn't be surprised if she lodged a complaint. But I had to. If I hadn't written it down, it would have been the only thing I focused on.

After five years in teaching (the last three at Hamilton), I knew her type. She would argue with me over every detail, a tiger mom of the first order. A lawyer lady in a suit that might as well have been a suit of armor. Hamilton Academy charged too much in tuition to allow their teachers to piss off the parents, so I had to handle these people pretty carefully. But that didn't mean I didn't enjoy proving that her daughter had plagiarized her paper.

Actually, I didn't enjoy it. Leigh Peacham had only been at Hamilton since the start of the school year and three weeks was hardly enough time to get to know a twelve-year-old, but the girl had impressed me as someone who was unusually bright and capable. She was settling in well and had become friends with two of the less-uptight girls in the class. The plagiarism was a surprise.

Warrior Mommy looked at the evidence, her brown eyes huge in her gamine face. This was a woman trying to look older than she was. How would she handle the situation?

She'd cursed. Mildly. I sort of liked her for that.

It was a slip in her hyperefficient demeanor. She might as well have said, *I thought I had everything under control, and now this. What the hell does this mean? What do I do about it? How did this happen?*

It sounded like the flute. Like pain laced with courage.

That melody was sliding around in my head. It had plenty of room. There were no other songs to compete with it.

She'd stalked out. I gave up believing I could finish grading these papers at school and threw my stuff into my backpack. As I cycled uptown, I kept hearing that melody. There was maybe a hint of percussion under it—the rhythm of angry heels in a long corridor?—and that worried me.

I'd made it to Harlem before I worked out *why* it worried me. (I didn't live in Harlem. You'd have to go further uptown to get to my crappy shoebox of an apartment. Harlem, like

Brooklyn before it, was now too expensive for anyone but tech hipsters.)

The problem was: if I was hearing music, then everything might come back.

The failed career.

Bump's unspoken hope that I'd pull it together again.

Mom, alone and silently raging in her pastel, soundly constructed retirement community, so unlike her beloved, creaky farmhouse.

Could I face all that disappointment again?

The future. *Let it grow, let it show.* Shudder.

Like I said, numb was easier. I could spend the rest of my life teaching kids about science. I could maintain peace and tranquility in my shoebox, a depressing apartment where I'd never have to take the current love interest (a parent at Hamilton—not, I would rush to point out, the mommy of one of *my* students—who'd told me after we were dating a while that she was married and thus as interested as I was in keeping our relationship as clandestine and emotionless as possible).

A flute melody I could ignore. One flute was a solo performer. But percussion meant Bump. It meant a band.

It meant possibly failing others again, as well as myself.

Typically, my ride home filled me with energy. Late September was a gorgeous time in New York City, and I absolutely loved biking past traffic jams. I loved the Big Apple, but I was an environmentalist too. As long as everyone insisted on riding around in cars, most with only one person in each gas-guzzling monster, then we were going to waste time and resources in traffic jams—and bike riders like me were going to feel holier-than-thou. Rightly so.

Today I'd peddled past angry, shouting faces without

giving them more than surface attention. Over the bridge, past Yankee Stadium, deep into the Bronx, and I realized I was cycling to the melody. It wasn't going to let me go.

I chained my bike to a pole outside the Morris Heights Deli—situated in the sylvan paradise of trash and chain link fencing under the Cross Bronx Expressway—and took the front wheel in with me. Bump was working behind the counter, stocking the case with fruit sodas and energy drinks.

"Fonse," he called when he saw me. "Bart's here."

A dark-haired streak shot out of the kitchen. Alfonso, son of Bump's girlfriend, Pandora, was nine. He avoided crashing into me but only by grabbing my arm and swinging me around. "Do you have it?" he cried.

"I got it, I got it. Calm down."

Pandora appeared in the kitchen pass-through, and Bump came to watch. I opened my backpack and pulled out the tablet. Fonse was dancing with impatience. "Let me see!"

I showed him how the cover opened into a keyboard.

"And this will hook me up to the Hamilton PrimaryNet?"

"Once we set it up." I tried to help him establish an account, but the only thing he needed from me was the school-issued password. After that, the three adults watching him were simple hindrances. He moved as if in a dream to a table in the corner, and then we ceased to exist for him.

Pandora appeared at my elbow. "This isn't going to get you into trouble, is it?"

"Nah, I cleared it with the principal. The IT team set it up." I turned my back on the boy, though he wouldn't have noticed if Batman had come in to order a knish. "They'll be watching the browser history, so better not let anyone else use it."

"Use it?" Pandora wrinkled her cute brown nose. "We're not even taking that tablet out of the deli. It stays under lock and key, and that means it never goes home to Uncle Francisco. No worries there."

Pandora's cousin was a kind man, but the company he kept left something to be desired, and Pandora kept her boy near her whenever he wasn't in school. She moved to Fonse to review the rules with him about caring for the tablet. He listened with barely disguised impatience. Bump leaned over the counter, hiding a smile.

"What'll you have, O Great One?"

Goddamn it. I heard a bass line.

I blinked and tried to cover, but Bump's known me a long time. "Did you hear something?"

I must have looked like a deer in the headlights. He came out from behind the counter, a shambling bear of a man, and shook me.

"Bart! Did you just hear music?"

It hurt to hear how excited he was. Bump was the most patient person on the planet—a lot of pot will do that to you—but his dreams of being a musician were tied to my ambitions. And my ambitions had been silent for three years.

"Just a bass line," I admitted. I didn't dare tell him it was the second song I'd heard in the last two hours.

He whooped in glee. "A bass line is almost a drum line! We're back in business, baby!"

He grabbed me and lifted me off my feet. He tried to swing me in a circle, but my feet and shins kept knocking into chairs and tables and he dropped me again to the astonished gaze of Pandora, Fonse, and the boss's wife, Mrs. Chen, leaning in from her office in the kitchen.

"What?" Pandora asked.

"Nothing," Bump said, watching me carefully. "Not a

thing at all. Back away slowly. Let the man think." He was teasing me, but there was a core of truth to his reaction. "We don't want to force anything, here. Get this man a cheesesteak."

"Christ, do you want to kill me? Panda, can I have a veggie wrap? Extra cheese?"

"You can have the entire package," she said. "You're both crazy, but I love you." She kissed my cheek in passing and Bump pretended to be horrified. She goosed him before disappearing into the kitchen.

Bump regarded me carefully. "Been a long time, man."

"Might not be anything."

"I know. Hey, thanks for the tablet."

"He's a bright kid." We were temporarily alone, and I leaned in for a confidence. "I talked to them about bringing in Fonse's school to the PrimaryNet weather program. They said his school should apply, but there are already eight other schools lined up, and we probably won't raise enough money for all of them, much less a ninth."

"One thing at a time, brother." Bump nodded toward the kitchen. "Let me talk her into going to Fonse's teacher first. She's not too comfortable with the idea of promises that probably won't be kept."

"That kid needs a program like this."

"Tell me about it. He's been all over the weather since you told him about the Hamilton PrimaryNet. He was asking me math questions last night that I couldn't begin to answer, and I was an electrical engineer."

I grinned. "You were an electrical engineering student for two years until you flunked out and slept on my couch."

"Details. The point is, the kid's off the charts."

"I know."

I was finishing my veggie wrap, which was dripping in

melted cheese—always make the cook happy if you want a great meal—when I remembered the Warrior Mommy's comments.

"Bump, is there something wrong with my jeans?"

"Your jeans? Fuck if I know. You got something on them?"

"I don't know."

"Stand up. Turn around. No, they look fine."

"They look *fiiine*," Pandora called from the kitchen.

Mrs. Chen popped up long enough to agree. "Those are *niiiiice* jeans."

I was confused again. "What? They're from college. Is there a rip?"

"Turn around again," Mrs. Chen called. I presented my back to them, and Pandora and Mrs. Chen both applauded.

"Maybe they are a little tight," I hedged.

"They're perfect. Don't change a thing!" Pandora called, and Bump raised a threatening fist in her direction. "Your jeans are perfect, too, honey!"

Hmm. Maybe I'd invest in a few pairs of khakis.

4

GABBING WITH MY GIRLS

CALLIE

I'd missed dinner with Leigh again, thanks to Addie Belle the time narcissist. I'd had to rework my entire afternoon and then make my team stay late to make up the time. And Leigh was already in bed by the time I got home.

I thanked Mrs. Kim, sent her on her way, and then collapsed, too tired to even think about a restorative glass of wine.

The trees out the kitchen window were showing their fall colors in the sodium streetlights. New York was a reasonably green city. and our apartment on West Twelfth Street was low enough to have a leafy view. Even with the raise in my annual salary, I never would have been able to afford a two-bedroom in Manhattan if a company lawyer hadn't been deputized to Japan for two years. Addie Belle had grinned like a shark when she'd produced the sublet.

Even with the salary increase, money was tight. Money was always tight. My ex, West, paid no alimony (I'd been so eager to be rid of him, I didn't bother trying to try to squeeze blood from that stone) and his child-support payments were sporadic. I covered the cost of Hamilton Academy out of my salary, which didn't leave much left over for the sublet, Mrs. Kim, the payment on my student loans, and the debt West had run up.

And now I needed to find the time to run a school talent show.

I wasn't about to sink in my despair, but the water was getting deep. I texted my besties.

What are you guys up to?

Cleo answered quickly enough that she must have had her phone in her hand.

History channel. Bunkum. Need to talk it out?

Talk what out?

Whatever has you texting after bedtime.

She knew me so well.

Rita didn't bother texting. She just called.

"Hang on. Let me conference in Cleo," she said. I had an app on my phone that tracked Rita's location (with her permission, of course). Rita, a long-distance trucker, was driving down a highway in Kansas, probably a few miles over the posted speed limit, and setting up a conference call on her phone. That didn't seem safe. But Rita walked on the wild side. I offered to do it instead, but Cleo was already picking up.

"Evening, my sisters!" Cleo, an archivist for the US House of Representatives, was the motherly member of the trio. Rita was the id, all about urges and fulfillment. I suppose that made me the governor. The rule follower. The stick-in-the-mud.

"Hey, baby," Rita said. "Callie, spill it."

I protested with a laugh. "What? Can't we just talk?"

"Sure, we can—and we do. But not the evening after

you're summoned to Leigh's school for some infraction. Was she smoking pot? I bet she was smoking pot."

"Rita, no. She's twelve."

"Uh-huh. Like I said."

"Shush. Callie, what was the meeting about?" Gentle Cleo loved Leigh as much as Rita did.

I sighed and reviewed the meeting. Of course, Rita seized on the description of the biology teacher.

"A hot ass, huh? You should use that guy like a bar of soap, Callie. Be good for you after that scumbag you finally divorced."

"Oh, please!" I protested, my face warming from the blush they couldn't see. "Leigh has a crush on him. I'm not poaching from my daughter!"

"Of course you're not," Cleo soothed. "Have you talked to Leigh about the paper?"

"I'll do it tomorrow at breakfast. I missed dinner again." My girls heard my guilt and hastened to assure me that Leigh could handle a hardworking mother. "But that wasn't the most interesting thing about that meeting," I added. "My boss's wife, Addie Belle. You remember I told you about her?"

"The beauty queen," Rita said.

"Well, maybe not exactly a pageant winner, but you've got the right image. Anyway, she got me to agree to run the school's talent show in March. And she knows I'm swamped with this horrific military case at work."

"Mercenaries slaughtering civilians." Rita said it bluntly, but she wasn't wrong.

"That's the one. It's going to eat up all my time. But Lawrence apparently expects me to be able to do both, and Addie Belle couldn't wait to tell me so. Plus, I'm sorry to say that her expectations are sky-high. She draped a whole host of impossible conditions on me in the cloak of 'Hamilton traditions' and then dared me to object."

"Wow," Cleo said. "What are you going to do? Can we help?"

"Thank you, but with you in Washington and Rita all over North America, I think I have to put this one together without you."

"I don't like the sound of that," Rita said. "None of us are ever alone, you know? I count on you guys, and that means I count on you telling me when you need me. Hear me?"

Rita was all passion, all energy. Her loyalty was precious to me, and her insistence brought tears to my eyes. I blinked to clear my vision.

"I hear you, and I'll let you know if I need you to drop everything. But I won't. Now, tell me about Mimi and the house."

The three of us had met in college because we'd each rented space in a rickety Georgetown mansion from Mimi, a sweet old lady who became my pretend grandmother. West and I had rented her decrepit carriage house, and Rita and Cleo had both had rooms on the second floor.

"Well," Cleo said, "the news isn't great. The city sent a list of repairs that have to be made to stop them from declaring the house unfit for human habitation. I emailed a copy to you, Rita. Did you get a chance to look it over?"

Cleo was the only one who was still in DC, and she took on things like bill-paying for Mimi. Not that our grand-mother-by-choice had much in her bank account to pay those bills with.

"I saw it. I can do the gutters the next time I swing through, and we can replace the water heater ourselves." Rita, who came up to my shoulder and was as curvy and girly as a human could be, had a knack for mechanics neither Cleo nor I could match. "We've got some more expensive items we're going to need help with, though."

We frowned over money for a while. None of Mimi's "granddaughters" had much money. There was only so far our discussions could take us. "I still think we could persuade her to subdivide her land," I said. "Get her to sell off the garden. At Georgetown prices, she could realize enough to pay for all the repairs."

Both Rita and Cleo laughed, although it was with more sorrow than amusement. All three of us knew how much the garden meant to Mimi. "Not gonna happen," Rita said. "She loves that old tree and all those nooks and crannies in the backyard."

"I know." I sighed. "This is another knot I can't figure out how to untangle."

"Speaking of which," Cleo said. "Tell us about the case from hell. What's going on with mercenaries slaughtering civilians?"

"Ugh." I shuddered. Lawrence McCrillis had pulled me from the DC office because I had experience working on cases of federal law and, by virtue of a rape case in which an active-duty Marine was accused of assaulting a tourist in the back room of a Georgetown bar, on cases in collaboration with the Judge Advocate General's office (that is, military law).

AresCorp was Hoare Ascutney's largest client, a multinational corporation with deployments in active-duty military zones around the world. Rita and Cleo had the word mostly right. These people *would* have been called mercenaries in an earlier day. Today they were known as military contractors. The gray area of overlap between civilian and military law was a legal quandary, a ticking time bomb, and Hoare Ascutney had caught the first mighty fragments:

Two AresCorp operatives had gunned down seventeen men, women, and children in Syria. They'd insisted the group was armed and dangerous. Three local witnesses said the civilians were simply seeking a safe place to hide when two Americans had opened fire without warning.

So, we were dealing with international law in a nation where the United States had uncertain standing, with military law *and* with federal law. It was a mess.

"I'll deny it if asked," I confided, "but the more I look into the case, the more I secretly believe those two mercenaries are guilty as sin." Both of them looked exactly like the kind of men who should be kept far, far away from automatic weaponry. These experienced military contractors had left me with a creeping unease when I took their depositions, as if snakes in darkness were crawling over exposed skin.

"Shit," Rita swore.

"What are you going to do?" Cleo asked.

"My job." I sighed. "I'll make sure there are no legal grounds upon which to convict them—or, by extension, AresCorp."

"What's your hotshot new boss say about it?" Rita asked.

Lawrence, husband of Addie Belle, was the senior lawyer on the case. "He knows it's an ugly situation. When he pulled me from obscurity to work on this, he told me he was setting aside his personal feelings about the case to give our clients the best legal defense possible, despite their unsympathetic actions. He asked me if I could do the same."

"And you said you could." Cleo's voice was warm with support. She was so good to me.

"When I said I could, he shook my hand like he was proud of me. I'm hoping I've finally found a legal mentor. I swear, you guys, working with Lawrence is about the only silver lining in this dark cloud."

"It's going to work out," Cleo said. "It's all going to work out."

"And if it doesn't, we'll take a tire iron to the lot of them. Except the hottie with the tight ass. We're keeping him."

I burst out laughing, loving the sisterhood we'd formed, and then heard shuffling feet behind me.

"Mom," Leigh said sleepily. "What are you doing up?"

5

LATE-NIGHT CONVERSATIONS

CALLIE

"Baby, I'm sorry. Did I wake you?"

"I don't know," my daughter said with her customary directness. "Maybe. I don't know what woke me. Who are you talking to?"

Cleo and Rita both demanded Leigh-time, and our conversation took a less intense turn. I closed it down after a few minutes. "It's a school night. We've all got to get some sleep. You drive safely, Rita."

"I love you, Aunt Rita and Aunt Cleo!"

"We love you, too, sweetie!"

Digital hugs, kisses, promises to get together soon, and then Leigh and I were alone again in the peaceful serenity of the nighttime kitchen. My daughter looked at me with a wisdom far beyond her years—a wisdom that hurt my heart because it was borne from my terrible marriage. No child should have that much life experience.

"Are you all right?" she asked me.

She wanted to take care of me as much as I wanted to

take care of her. I smiled. "I'm fine, love. I just couldn't sleep."

She began moving around the kitchen. "I'll make you a sandwich. You're hungry."

"No, I'm not."

"Yes, you are."

I thought about it. She was right. I was hungry.

I watched her, unable to stop my proud smile. She wasn't a woman yet, but that was clearly right around the corner. Which reminded me.

"I met your bio teacher today."

Not very nice of me to sneak up on her like that when she was taking care of me, but it was a great cross-examination technique. Sure enough, she jumped and dropped a knife on the floor. Fortunately, she'd yet to dip into the mayo, so it wasn't a mess.

"You met Mr. Thetford? Why?"

"He wanted to talk to me about your paper."

She closed her eyes and then faced me, squaring her shoulders and giving me impressive eye contact. "You know I cheated."

That girl. I was crazy about her, but now wasn't the time to show it. "I do. Why? Why would you do something like that?"

She scrunched up her face. "You'll think I'm stupid."

"I've never thought you were stupid. Not even once. Tell me why."

I knew why. What I wanted to know was if she would still tell me. I could handle her growing up. I just wasn't sure I could handle her growing away from me.

She got leftover pork loin out of the fridge to slice it. "I like him," she said, and my heart beat again. She could still confide in me.

"Like him-like him?" I asked, clarifying unnecessarily.

She nodded. "I know it's silly. He's much older than me. But . . . I want him to think I'm smart."

"You are smart."

"Not that kind of smart. I mean—older. Like . . . someone he would want to talk to."

I nodded thoughtfully. "Well. You know cheating is wrong."

"I know."

"There have to be consequences."

She went on building my sandwich while she listened.

I went on. "No spending money. One hundred percent of your allowance goes into your savings account for the next four weeks, and you're grounded for two weeks. You must come home directly after school. No more shopping or trips to the park with Shane and Olivia."

"Shane's birthday party is on Saturday. May I still go to that?"

"You can go to the party and be grounded for three weeks or skip the birthday party and be grounded for two."

"I'll take the three weeks." She put the sandwich in front of me and slid into the chair next to me. "I'm sort of relieved. I don't like cheating. I'm apparently not very good at it."

I couldn't hide my smile entirely. "Life is easier when you're honest," I agreed. "Mr. Thetford is giving you what he calls your 'only possible Get Out of Jail Free card.' You've got two days to submit a paper you actually wrote, and he'll delete the plagiarized one."

"I've already written it. I had it when I cheated with the other one. I'll turn it in tomorrow."

"I'm sure he'll be impressed by that."

She picked at the table, not looking at me. "What did you think of him?" she asked diffidently.

"Cute," I replied. She grinned, still not willing to look at me. "I'm afraid I made a rather rude comment about his bee-hind."

That got her attention. Horror and joy warred on her face. "No! What did you say?"

"Asked him if he wore those jeans in front of his students."

"I love those jeans!"

"I can see why."

"What'd he say?"

"I don't think he acknowledged it at all. Is he a good teacher?"

"Oh, he's great. He makes bio really easy to understand. We did the coolest experiment yesterday."

She was off on a long explanation. I let her eager enthusiasm wash over me, warm with the knowledge that she was still mine.

It's hard for a twelve-year-old to be trapped in her parents' bitter divorce, and Leigh wanted to take care of me as much as she wanted to care for her father. I worried about how she was handling it. There were times when she seemed too adult. Too capable.

So, this foray into adolescent crushes and cheating was, in a way, reassuring.

I knew I leaned on her too much. She was my daughter, not my best friend. Cleo and Rita held that place, even if they were too far away now. Once, there'd been another friend who'd turned out to be a terrible betrayer, typified by the fact that she'd changed her name from Susan to Cayenne and moved in with my ex-husband.

But that didn't matter anymore. I didn't need friends nearby, and I would be a loving and supportive mother to my child. I would pay off the massive student loans and the whopper of a credit card bill that West had saddled me with. I'd win the AresCorp case and then donate my time in pro bono work at a legal clinic to wash my soul clean.

And I'd put on a damned talent show. Wince.

"Hey. Mrs. McCrillis wants me to run the talent show."

Leigh raised her eyebrows. "That's a really big deal at Hamilton. It's all the kids are talking about."

"Well, I've got six months to pull it together."

"Isn't that when you thought the AresCorp thing was going to trial?"

"About then, yes, so I've got to get organized."

"You *are* organized."

"More organized, then."

"Good luck with that!"

"You're helping me."

"I am?"

"You're my man on the ground. We have to round up talent, so keep your eyes open."

"Can I make a video for the talent show?"

"You mean show a video instead of sing or do a tap dance or something?" I was doubtful. Videos weren't on Addie Belle's list of acceptable performance options . . . but neither were they specifically prohibited. "Sure," I said stoutly. "Let's make this our talent show. Make a video."

She nodded decisively. "I'll make it about the Hamilton PrimaryNet. That's such a cool idea—all these primary schools linked across the state to track weather systems. I'll start storyboarding tomorrow."

A chip off the old block. Impulsively, I pulled her to me in a hug. She smelled wonderful. Like home. The happiest part of home.

She drew back after a moment. "You should get Mr.

Thetford to help! He can sing. I heard he does shows and concerts."

"Really? He's a musician?"

"He says he's going to bring his guitar on the field trip on Tuesday. We're having a bonfire on the beach, and he says every bonfire needs a guitar."

"All right, then Tuesday will be his audition. He won't know it, though."

"I bet he can really sing. Don't you love the way he rumbles when he talks? He's got a great voice."

"Huh," I replied in noncommittal agreement. I'd admit that I was biased against artists of all stripes and was sorry to see her interest in a musician.

My grandmother had married a plumber. He turned out to paint portraits in his spare time. He wasn't bad at it either. He also ran a floating craps game in Paramus, New Jersey. After a few decades, the cops got tired of chasing him and they locked him up for a while. My gran had raised my mother pretty much by herself.

Then my mother fell for a trumpet player. Beautiful man. Lovely father—to me, and to two other families we'd discovered so far. He wasn't talking, but he spent a lot of time on the road. Could've been more wives and more half brothers and sisters out there. By virtue of being the first of his many wives, Mom had gotten to keep the name, but she'd dumped the guy. It had been hard on her—and on me.

And I'd been no smarter. I'd made it to college a year ahead of schedule, and at seventeen was no match for the beautiful sculptor hiring live models for his Drawing 101 class. Any psychologist worth his salt would tell you I was trying to replace my daddy, and West was every bit as charming (and almost as old) as my father.

We married as soon as I realized I was pregnant. West had been thrilled with Leigh, saying I was his muse and Leigh was his mini muse. I'd taken out student loans to finish college and then gone to Georgetown Law while West took care of Leigh. Later, I realized he was also taking care of half the ladies in the neighborhood. The only females he didn't proposition were Cleo and Rita.

During the divorce, Leigh told me she'd once had to summon an Uber when she was nine because West had brought her with him to his current paramour's house. West and the lover had gotten drunk and passed out. Leigh had gotten herself home and was in bed, teeth brushed, face washed, and sound asleep by the time I got home. She didn't tell me at the time because she didn't want to worry me. When she did tell me, I cried for so long that my mother insisted on tranquilizers.

So, there was a pattern here. The women in my family fell for gorgeous artists who inevitably let them down, sometimes quite painfully. My mother once confided that Dad had given her a dose of the clap. When she learned that West had been unfaithful (again and again and again), she advised I get tested for every known STI. Luckily, I was clean. Of course, West and I had slept together less and less as the years went on. He'd felt I was ignoring him, and I'd been too tired.

It had been a while for me, sexually—not that I was looking. I barely had time for the challenges already laid before me. I wasn't taking on the burdens and nuisances of a man too. The qualities of the bio teacher's deep voice were of little interest to me.

"Come on, baby girl. Tomorrow is going to be here before we know it. Let's get some sleep." Her hand slipped into mine as we left the kitchen. "Thanks for the sandwich," I said.

"Sleep in my bed tonight," she replied. "You'll sleep better."

We reset her alarm to wake me at six. She was right. I slept better with my darling daughter curled up at my side.

6

THE DAILY GRIND

CALLIE

By noon, I stupidly thought I'd gotten my hands around the situation.

I had spreadsheets and color-coded schedules and efficient tip tables. I allocated the resources to simultaneously handle both a major lawsuit and a ridiculous talent show. I was on top of things . . . until conditions suddenly went from "I barely have enough time but can manage it" to "I am definitely screwed."

I was sitting in my office on the seventy-third floor of Hoare Ascutney's world headquarters. It wasn't a particularly nice office; I was miles away from the nearest window and had to access webcams to determine the weather outside.

(The weather was becoming a theme in my life. Currently? The midday sky was gray, and rain was reflecting neon up and down Sixth Avenue. Kids at my daughter's school were probably tracking the rain through their as-yet one-station network. All I knew was that it was a good day to be tucked, safe and dry, deep inside this rabbit warren with the building's deli on speed dial. Kale salad with salmon for lunch today, half eaten and pushed aside to make room for a sea of research on relevant—and, alas, irrelevant—international case law.)

My office in DC had been bigger and had a window, but space was cheaper in Washington than it was in Manhattan. This one could have been worse. It was a full office, with walls to the ceiling and a door that shut, not a cubicle. I'd intended to frame a photo of Leigh to put up, along with my diplomas, but there hadn't been time yet. My walls were bare, which left room for a Post-it note schedule that we could move around as events shifted in the AresCorp case. It wasn't particularly pleasing, aesthetically, but it was immensely practical.

And my office on the seventy-third floor was on the same floor as my boss, Lawrence McCrillis. My team of four junior associates and a varying pool of nervous law school interns were grouped in cubes around my door, so I had a mini fiefdom going. I could work with it.

Perhaps most strategically, from my door (currently open to keep an eye on my team, who were inclined to slack off if not held to the grindstone), I could see the hallway leading from reception into the inner workings—down which Lawrence himself was now strolling, with his wife, Addie Belle, clinging to his arm.

Dispassionately, I noted that she was doing her Dominate from Weakness thing, where she was letting him think he was leading her down the hall and not the other way around.

Addie Belle was cradling a huge book of fabric samples. She was redoing Lawrence's corner suite. I'd been reliably informed by Carla, one of the junior associates on my team, that this was the third time in two years. Scuttlebutt was that she liked to keep an eye on things at Hoare Ascutney. Since she was spoken of with both reverence and fear, I had to respect her ability to manipulate. Leading from behind, indeed.

Lawrence looked up and saw me. His handsome older face broke into a smile. "There she is!" he cried with warmth.

I fixed a welcoming smile on my face while thinking, What fresh new hell is this?

The pair stopped in my door, and Lawrence reached in to shake my hand as I stood. "My Addie tells me your remarkable news!"

I looked my question at him politely.

He went on. "Taking on the school's talent show *and* the AresCorp case? My god, Callie, are you superhuman?"

Surprised, I looked at Addie Belle, whose expression clearly showed that she shared her husband's awed astonishment.

"I th-thought—" I stuttered.

Weakness. Must stop sputtering immediately.

Addie Belle cut me off. "I told Lawrence you insisted on taking on the whole thing yourself. He was so impressed, weren't you, darling?"

"I was, indeed. That's the biggest event at the school! It'll take a lot of your time. Are you sure you can do that *and* tackle AresCorp?"

I looked at Addie Belle and judged her sweet smile the way I'd assess a juror. I found her too sweet by half. A false face if ever I'd seen one.

"Absolutely, Lawrence," I said, doubling down on Addie's unspoken challenge. "I can handle both. You won't even notice."

He crowed with approval. "You, my girl, are a real go-getter!"

Addie's smile seemed to sour a fraction, and I knew a quiet burst of satisfaction. She'd thought I'd cave.

The hell I would.

"Why don't we make this exciting?" Lawrence said. Addie Belle and I were equally interested in the next words out of his mouth. "How much did the fundraiser make last year, Addie?" he asked her.

"Why, darlin', I think they pulled in over a million dollars last year."

"Pretty good for an elementary school, don't you think?" He looked to me to make sure I shared his pride in one of the most elite day schools in the nation managing to squeeze a million out of their mover-and-shaker parents. I nodded obediently. "You beat that total *and* help us crush the AresCorp charges, and I'll get you an office with a window." He grinned at me, aware (as the entire office was aware) that only partners got window offices.

Partner. Before I turned thirty.

Again, my response was less a choice and more an inevitability. "Done," I said promptly. "Start picking who you're going to move out now."

He was delighted with my brio. Addie Belle was less so. I could hear my team listening eagerly to every word from their cubicles, already tapping phones and keyboards to spread the hot news.

Addie handed Lawrence the binder of fabric swatches. "Take these to your office, will you, lover? I'm going to cover a few thoughts about the talent show with our sweet Callie, here."

You had to admire her skill. He was one of the most

powerful, impressive lawyers on the planet, and she'd dismissed him like a butler. He left, grinning and happy.

Addie was not so foolish as to have a conversation in front of an open door. Unlike her husband, she didn't see the staff as employees to be moved like chess pieces. She knew they were witnesses. She secured her privacy by closing the door before sweeping around the desk to sit primly in my chair, leaving me standing before her like a supplicant.

Two could play that game. I braced my hands on the desk, looming over her. "What's going on? You told me Lawrence approved my taking on the talent show."

She smiled smugly. "Did I? I meant that I intended to ask him. He was very startled when I told him at lunch." She dropped her Sweet Southern Miss act and flexed to bring out her talons. "You're going to fail, Callie, darlin'. Go back to Washington now, before you get hurt."

Analytically, I assessed her statement. A clear threat.

She expected me to be startled, hoping she could scare me. I swiveled so I was sitting on the edge of my desk, towering over her and invading her personal space. "Why?" I asked simply.

She blinked, masking surprise. A point for me.

"I keep what I want," she said.

"I don't want anything you have."

She expressed scorn with a single arched eyebrow and a tiny huff. "Everyone wants what I have. But you're not getting him."

"Lawrence? You think I want *Lawrence*? Addie—he's old." My surprise made me careless with my words.

She came to her feet with a rush, and I was the one thrown off-balance.

"Old? He's *powerful*. And you want that." She snapped

her fingers at me. "But you can't have him. And he can't have you."

She pushed past me and headed for the door.

"He doesn't want me," I tried, but her scorn was even more evident this time.

"You're going to fail, Callie. I'll see to it. There is no office with a window in your future. Not in this building. Not in this city."

She touched the doorknob and her transformation was remarkable. By the time she'd pulled it open, her sweet smile was as firmly fixed as if she never lost it. "All right, darlin', I'll let you know when the board meets. We can decide all that then. Toodles!"

She'd gotten the last word. Damn it.

It was a gorgeous power play, and I had to respect her for it.

But without a doubt, I had somehow managed to acquire an enemy. I was now screwed.

Lawrence was in meetings all afternoon and couldn't speak with me until seven. I spent the rest of the day terrorizing my team. By the time I got his ear, I was determined to have advanced the AresCorp case by a week at least.

Of course, the moment I disappeared into Lawrence's office, every single one of my team scattered like cockroaches, fleeing to their homes, where they no doubt drank Scotch heavily and bitched about their insane virago of a team leader. Traitors.

Well, enjoy your evening, fellows. I was looking at at least six hours of research into how to run a fundraiser before I got to go home. And I needed to call my adopted grandmother to reason with her. As predicted, Mimi had flat-out refused to consider subdividing her land and selling the garden. If we didn't do something, her home would be condemned. Add it to the list of things to deal with.

Lawrence was seated on the handsome tweed-and-leather sofa. His office was currently decorated to look like the viciously expensive library of a British country estate, if the estate featured panoramic floor-to-ceiling views of some of the most glittering, expensive real estate in the world.

Sunsets from this office were usually spectacular. Not tonight, though. The bleak clouds darkened the evening, and the low light and rain created an immediate intimacy in the vast office.

I perched next to Lawrence on the adjoining chair. He offered me a drink; I declined. Business as usual.

"I hope I haven't overstepped, volunteering for the talent show," I began. "Do you think I should back out of it?"

He shook his head. "Too late, Callie. They're counting on you now. Besides, if you pull this off? You'll be the toughest, most capable associate we've ever had. Not that I ever doubted you!"

Yep. I'd gotten myself in deep. There wasn't going to be an easy out.

"I'll assign you two more junior associates, though. You're going to need the help."

I bit back a denial. It was a weakness of mine, always wanting to tackle things on my own. He was right. My team was already muttering. If I wanted to avoid a full mutiny, I'd need more bodies to act as cannon fodder.

We went over the AresCorp case. It was my goal to be ahead of him on his requests, handing over information as soon as he asked for it. In the initial weeks since I'd been assigned to the case, I'd accomplished the goal three times —and each time felt like I'd gotten a gold star.

This evening, I proved that I'd outplanned him twice more. Two glorious times, he suggested an avenue of investigation and I showed him we'd already pursued it. Both times, Lawrence praised me. He reviewed the results with growing respect.

Maybe I wouldn't execute my team first thing when I made partner.

Not *first* thing, anyway.

"I was right about you," Lawrence said with a smile. "You *were* the right man for this job."

Compliments are tricky for a woman in this world. You have to look modest—but not too modest. If he'd praised a man, that man would have preened and been cocky, which was the more powerful response. I had to imply modest and show cockiness so he'd know I was someone to be reckoned with.

"That's true," I said. "I am. Of course, the right man is sometimes a woman."

Feminism. Gotta speak up when you can.

He threw back his head, his leonine, white hair pooling at his collar, and laughed. "Good for you!" he said.

And then his well-manicured, powerful hand landed on my knee.

Caution lights lit up across my brain. What the devil was this?

Don't overreact. It might be nothing. He might pat a male colleague's knee this way. *Well done, Bob*, he might say.

"But I don't think anyone would doubt for a minute that you're a woman!"

Yellow caution lights blinked red and then brightened to

a steady crimson when his fingers slid higher and curled around my leg above the knee, squeezing gently.

No doubt about it—if he did that to a male colleague, Bob would assume he was looking for a little spice on the down-low.

"Lawrence," I began.

He stopped me, pulling his hand away. "Don't look so panicked, Callie. We maintain the interdictum against defecating in places of mastication."

Cute. Don't shit where you eat.

"So," he went on, "you'll simply have to think about the possibilities until the AresCorp case is over. After that, you and I can have a discussion. Because I am impressed with you."

He looked at me intensely, his patrician-blue eyes gazing over his territory like a king.

See, this was exactly why fraternization in the military was forbidden. One person was always a higher rank than the other, and that meant the lower-ranked party felt pressure to please the higher-ranked party. Abuse was too easy.

Somehow, I was paralleling my initial conversation with his wife at the school. This, too, was a damned-if-you-do-damned-if-you-don't situation. I didn't want to encourage Lawrence. Not only did I not want to have an affair with him, but I'd recently learned that his wife was crazy enough to take it out of my hide.

But I didn't want to outright reject him either. I needed his help and patronage at Hoare Ascutney.

If he was willing to delay our "talk" until after the AresCorp case was settled, then I would have roughly half a year to deal with it. I'd figure it out. Somehow.

So, I summoned a smile and made it a warm one. "I'm flattered, Lawrence. We'll talk when the case is settled."

He winked at me as easily as if he winked every day at underlings he was propositioning—maybe he did—and then I was graciously dismissed.

Damn it.

Damn it. Addie was right. Lawrence did want me. I was *definitely* screwed.

7

HAVE KAYAK, WILL TRAVEL

BART

"Thanks for the ride, man."

I was slumped in the front seat of Bump's car, a disreputable Chrysler LeBaron that belched blue smoke but never failed to turn over. Reliable as death and taxes.

Behind the wheel, Bump brushed aside my gratitude. "Where's your truck, dude?"

"Still in Jersey. Same place."

"How long since you started it?"

I shrugged, looking out the window to end the conversation. It didn't work.

"When was the last time you went to see your mother?"

"Dunno." My grunt was spoken to the river. Bump feared no high-speed roadway in his rolling Detroit rusted steel, and we were cruising down the Henry Hudson Parkway from the Bronx, heading to Hamilton Academy in lower Manhattan.

"You should go see her, Bart."

"You go see her. She likes you better."

From the back seat, Fonse looked up from his book. He

often monitored conversations when we stupidly assumed he was lost in the pages. "Why doesn't Bart want to see his mom?" the boy asked.

"Good question," Bump said, glaring at me. "Got an answer?"

"She doesn't like me much," I said to the boy.

This was interesting enough for the boy to close his book, although one finger kept his place. "Why not? What did you do?"

I sighed. "It's complicated, Fonse."

"I like complicated."

"What are you reading?"

"About the Punic Wars. It's good." The distraction, however, was not successful. "Did you make her mad or something?"

"Punic Wars." I shook my head. "What are the Punic Wars?"

"Between Carthage and the Roman Empire. Did you make her mad?"

I tried one more time. "Where was Carthage? Is that, what, Italy?"

Fonse snorted in disgust. "Not Italy. A lot of places. The boundaries changed. What about your *mom*?" he insisted.

I shook my head and addressed the darkened window once more. "She wanted me to be a dairy farmer. I wanted to be a musician."

"And now you're a teacher. So, neither of you got what you wanted."

Damned kid. I could feel my eyebrows almost touching, I was so grumped by the conversation. "Thanks, Fonse. That's a good perspective on the situation."

"Lay off him, Fonse," Bump said mildly. "Not everyone has a mother as sweet and beautiful as yours."

Fonse snorted and turned back to his book.

"The kid's nine," I complained.

"I know," Bump said consolingly.

"You need a better school," I said to the back seat.

"I know," the back seat said.

We rolled on, covering in moments what took almost an hour on my ten-speed. It was quiet for a bit, and then the boy spoke from the darkness of the back seat.

"Why can't I go on the field trip again?"

He made me grin. I loved the way his mind worked. "First, because you don't go to Hamilton Academy."

The silence from the back seat was a judgment.

"Second, because you have school tomorrow."

"Hamilton Academy has school tomorrow, and they get to go."

"Only the seventh and eighth grades, which would not include you even if you did go there. And that's third."

"Grumph." The boy made an unintelligible sound of disapproval. "I have never been to Jamaica Bay. I have never been kayaking. You should take me."

"Okay," I said amicably. "Bump has a two-man kayak. We'll take that."

"Wait, where am I going to be?" Bump asked, annoyed.

"You want to come?" I asked.

"Yes." Bump feigned great affront.

"Then we'll need to find a way to strap both kayaks to the top of this heap."

"We've done it before."

"Maybe this weekend, Fonse."

The boy spoke gravely. "I'd rather skip school, but if this weekend is the best you can do, I can manage that."

"Thanks." I tried to match his seriousness, but I was sure he heard me laughing.

"Do I have to wear rubber pants with boots attached?" Fonse poked suspiciously at the pile of rubber lying next to him on the back seat.

"They're called hip waders. Nah, I wear those so I can load the kids into the kayaks without freezing to death. You can go in jeans and sneakers."

"Good. How many birds will you see tomorrow?"

I recognized the signs of the boy beginning a quiz and rolled my eyes. "I don't know. It's migratory season. I imagine quite a few."

"How many bird species does the National Park Service say can be found in the Jamaica Bay Wildlife Refuge?"

"I don't know."

"You're the teacher. You have to know."

"How many?"

"Three hundred and twenty-five. How many fish?"

I spent the rest of the drive alternately frustrated and delighted by Fonse. The boy was a continual source of amazement to me. Like a cowbird rolling its egg into an unsuspecting songbird's nest to care for it, Fonse had sprouted in a reasonably unintellectual family, who saw him as a highly lovable curiosity. The whole neighborhood watched Fonse with fascination.

We got to the school and Bump parked in the turn-around. I slung the backpacker guitar over my shoulder and fished out my door key. Bump untied the one-man kayak from the roof. "Can you get the waders?" I asked Fonse.

The boy hefted them with a martyred air but forgot to look aggrieved as he watched me open the door. "How far do we have to go with this stuff?"

"Just far enough to leave the kayak. I'll load it into the catering truck tomorrow before we go."

"Catering truck," Bump said, carefully without judgment.

"Can't have Manhattan's darlings eating sandwiches out of baggies," I supplied. "We've got a beachside clambake on order for tomorrow."

"Damn, boy, I want to go to this school." Bump looked like he couldn't decide whether to be annoyed or envious. "Like, with clams and corn on the cob?"

"And drawn butter and icebox cake."

"I don't like clams," Fonse said decidedly. "Let's go look at the weather station."

That was why he'd come, and I didn't mind bringing him in. The custodial staff knew me. Security had come to check us out when the door opened. Once they'd cleared me, they wouldn't care where in the school we went.

I gave my drummer and his almost-son a tour. Fonse was fascinated. We hit the roof to look at the equipment. I tried to explain what it was, but he'd already done his own research. Then we went to the meteorology lab set up in Mrs. Herring's room, and the boy was lost in study. Bump and I found a quiet moment for a chat.

"Doesn't Fonse have an uncle who could pay for him to come to a school like this?" I asked.

"Sure. Francisco. But it's money from various criminal enterprises, and Panda won't touch it."

"I guess that's best, but—"

"Yeah. The kid would flourish here. No more getting beat up for being too smart."

"Well," I hedged. "Rich kids are no kinder to the oddballs than poor ones are. Sometimes worse. But maybe less violent." I thought about it. "Maybe."

"Still, there might be teachers here who wouldn't mind when a kid knows as much as they do. Or more."

"That's true."

"It's too bad. That Francisco is a hell of a nice guy. But, you know—"

"—a gang leader."

"Yeah."

"No body parts in his freezer or anything? I thought all gangbangers had to be violent."

"Maybe. I've never seen anything. He'd love to pay for the kid too. He's always looking for a way to turn illegal money into something good for the family. Poor Pan. She's constantly having to turn down things she needs."

"She's strong."

"Strong as hell."

"Going okay with you guys, then."

It was a noncommittal statement that Bump could expand on if he wanted to. He didn't. "Yep."

"S'good."

We both nodded, hands in our pockets, watching Fonse explore the NOAA training program. Then it was my turn in the crosshairs.

"Heard any music lately?" Bump asked.

I shifted uneasily. The flute melody had been joined by a definite bass line and the start of a powerful chorus. Was I ready to admit it?

"Um," I said.

"Ah."

"Yeah."

"Okay. We wait."

Old friends, I thought, are without a doubt the best friends—and Bump was one of the most patient in the world. My drummer nudged me, shoulder to shoulder.

"They're having a UVM mini reunion in mid-November

at a coffeehouse in Chelsea. They want Bump and the Boys to get back together for it."

I stretched my neck awkwardly and considered how I felt about that. Strangely, I found I was less reluctant than usual to revisit past glories. It might even be fun if we could get Saul, Ajay, and Winston, the three other "boys" who made up the band.

"You want to do it?" I asked Bump.

"Hell yeah, I do. You?"

I thought about it. I did. "Okay. Let's set it up."

Bump tried to hide his grin in his beard, but I saw it anyway. It scared me—more people to disappoint—and pleased me at the same time. Feeling awkward, I called out to Alfonso, "Come on, kid, let's get back. It's nearly your bedtime."

"Coming."

8

ALL-CLASS FIELD TRIP

CALLIE

The Jamaica Bay Wildlife Refuge was a terrible place for conference calls.

It was pretty enough. Gorgeous, in fact—wetlands and golden grasses and sparkling waterways with the Manhattan skyline in the background.

The problem was the noise. Jamaica Bay lay at the foot of LaGuardia Airport, and a huge plane, low enough to rattle the fillings in my teeth, was taking off or landing about every thirty seconds.

So, I was huddled at a picnic table, my back to the serene beauty behind me, one hand clamped over my earpiece in an effort to hear my team. We were trying to explore all the possible ways I could interview the three witnesses to the incident in Syria. Could we get them a satellite phone for a phone deposition? Was there a local lawyer we could trust to do it for us without prejudice? Would I have to sneak into Syria and do it myself?

I was beginning to think that was the least complicated

option when I felt a tap on my shoulder. A timid woman stood behind me. “Mrs. Peacham?”

“Ms. Lyndon,” I replied. “But I am Leigh Peacham’s mother. Call me Callie.”

She smiled gratefully. “It’s time, Callie. Our class’s turn at the kayaks.”

I put my team on hold. “No, I’m just a driver,” I said. “I’m not going in the kayaks. I have a conference call.” I gestured uselessly to my headpiece and the laptop open on the table in front of me.

“Oh,” she said nervously. “I think you mean transportation.” She looked over her shoulder to where Addie Belle stood, her scarf tied jauntily through the belt loops of her perfect jeans. Addie Belle nodded encouragement to the woman.

“Right,” I said. “I’m a driver.”

“Well, no.”

I couldn’t force her to spit it out. I waited while she summoned the courage to set my misunderstanding aright.

“Transportation means the kayak too. You can swim, can’t you?”

Lord. I needed this time. “I can swim.”

“Oh, good!” She was relieved. “Then you can take one of the kayaks for our class.” She consulted her clipboard. “Yes, you’re to take Leigh and Olivia. Are you ready?”

I summoned patience. “I’m ready. Give me two minutes.”

“Safety talk begins in five. We’ll be right over there.” She gestured to where the kayak concessionaires were gathering kids and parents and distributing life jackets.

My team of associates and interns was all-too-obviously thrilled when I was forced to end the call. I needed to do something to pull them together. Promising not to execute them probably wouldn’t be enough. I’d have to tell them I’d get them all promotions if I made partner. That might help with their attitudes. Carrot and stick, threats and bribes.

My attitude, however, wasn't setting any new standards. My spirit could have used a shot of vitamin D or something. I stood at the back of the group and grumpily analyzed the safety demonstration, thinking idly of how I could bankrupt the kayak company based on their casual delivery of what should have been a tight, litigation-proof information session. Even the waivers we signed were crying out to be tested in court.

I kept my internal poison to myself until they handed me a ziplock baggie. "What's this for?"

"Anything you don't want to get wet," the guy said, gesturing to my earpiece. "I'm guessing there's a phone to go with that. Is it waterproof?"

"You said the kayaks wouldn't flip."

"I said they probably wouldn't flip. You want to risk it? Or you can leave it here."

Leave my phone? Unlikely. I zipped my electronics into my pocket. I'd already left my laptop with the caterers.

"All right. Now what?"

Leigh pointed happily to where two of the concession guys and Mr. Thetford were standing up to their knees in the water, holding long kayaks steady as two classmates and one adult each clambered carefully in from a low dock. "Come on!"

Leigh had become inseparable with her two friends. Olivia had dyed half her dark hair with a strawberry froth, and Shane's mom had sprung for the full rainbow for her daughter's blonde head. With Leigh's shiny turquoise, they were an adorable trio. Shane was already loading into her kayak, and Olivia and Leigh were with me.

Of course, the girls made sure we ended up being

helped into our kayak by Mr. Thetford, dressed in a disreputable pair of waist-high waders held up by saggy suspenders. The two guys from the kayak concession were in sleek wet suits. They looked like spies, while Mr. Thetford looked like Uncle Pete Fishes For Trout In The River—if Uncle Pete had a shaggy head of hair and an adorable smile.

Leigh and Olivia were all but cooing with happiness as he helped them slide into the kayak.

"Okay, Mom," he said, looking up. "Now you. Oh." He recognized me, even though I'd dressed casually in jeans and a sweatshirt for the occasion. No corporate shark getup for me today. "Mrs. Lyndon. Nice to see you again."

"Ms.," I said awkwardly, sitting on the dock and attempting to slither into the kayak with any grace at all. "I'm not a Mrs." I knew Addie Belle, from her command post by the catering truck, would be watching me try to get into the kayak. Watching and smiling.

His hand was all that kept me from sliding ingloriously into the water between the dock and the boat. "I just can't get your name right, huh?"

"Call me Callie," I said automatically. Then, because that was an odd thing to say to my daughter's bio teacher, I focused intensely on the foot pedals that steered the craft.

"You understand how they work?" he asked, leaning down. He smelled of fresh air and the slight saltiness of the marshes. I stopped sniffing him.

"Theoretically."

"It's pretty easy. If you have trouble, you can steer with these." He handed us each the long, double-bladed paddles. "Girls, you know what you're looking for."

"Evidence of the food web," Leigh said from her spot in the front.

"Right. Fish, insects, bivalves, reptiles, birds—see if you

can see signs of any mammals. Keep your eyes open. You've got an hour. When you hear my whistle, head back so the next class can go. We'll seine the water after lunch. Okay, have fun."

He pushed us away gently, and we were left to figure out what we were doing on our own.

It took a few minutes, but Olivia and I soon learned to time our strokes to Leigh's so we were all pulling together. Mr. Thetford was right: the foot pedals were easy to use, although the boat turned more slowly than I'd expected.

It wasn't long before we were moving surprisingly quickly. The view was astonishing. We were lost in the wetlands in moments, surrounded on all sides by the sound of the grasses rustling in the gentle breeze and the laughter of other classmates as they navigated channels and pushed off mudbanks.

Leigh and Olivia were enchanted. They heard a bird call, a squeaking, wild sound, and insisted we follow the sound to see if we could identify it.

From my seat in the back, I found I was relaxing. The rhythm of the paddling was nice. No, better than nice. Excellent.

No, better than that. It was *wonderful*. I made a smooth gesture and we pulled through the water. My shoulders, my neck, my back, my abs—all parts of me were working in harmony, and my tension was somehow left back on land. Stress was leaving me with even greater efficiency than my pre-bedtime workout on the elliptical. I wanted more.

We came to a fork in the waterway. "Want to go left or right, Leigh?"

"I don't know," she said. "I'm not sure. I wish the bird would call again."

"Indecision is the killer," I told her. "There're no wrong choices, but you have to make a choice."

From behind me, I heard a startled noise. I turned and found Mr. Thetford in his one-man kayak, paddling near us. He looked at me in surprise.

"She's right," he said, and then he was fumbling in his vest pockets for something—pen and paper, as it turned out. The man was constantly stopping to scribble things, I thought.

"Okay. Let's go left!"

"You got it. Lead on. We'll take the rhythm from you."

From behind me, he laughed shortly, and then we were in the channel and slipping easily along a sparkling waterway.

"Look!" Olivia cried. "What's that bird?"

We drifted instead of paddling, heading toward a brown, long-legged bird on a mud flat. As we watched, it held out its wings to the sides and uttered the wild, squeaking call again.

"That's a curlew," Mr. Thetford said from behind us. "Good spotting. What can you tell about it from its appearance?"

Olivia and Leigh offered their thoughts and he worked with them, floating alongside us and using easy questions to suggest new avenues of investigation. He helped them narrow down the possibilities from the available clues until they decided that curlews lived on mud flats, hunted for worms and insects with their curving beaks, and were probably good fliers.

His method for working them closer and closer to a sound observation was rather like how I approached a legal case, and as soon as I realized that, I discovered a possible strategy for deposing our Syrian witnesses.

We needed to get them to Jordan. They might even appreciate the chance to get out of the country.

This presented a thousand challenges, but also many opportunities. My hand went to my phone and Mr. Thetford looked around, started by my sudden movement.

I stopped. It would wait.

Agonizing as it might be, it could wait.

"Are you enjoying yourself?" he asked kindly.

"I am," I responded, surprising myself with the depths of my sincerity. "It's like sitting right on top of the water."

"Like a water bug," he agreed happily. "The cell reception's pretty crappy once you get away from the landing anyway."

He laughed at my astonishment—he'd read me that easily?—and then paddled off to check in with other kayakers.

Leigh and Olivia chose where to go; I simply provided the muscle. The hour flew by. I wasn't as relaxed as I'd been, now itching to get going on my investigation, but the paddling continued to fill me with a sense of strength and rightness. When the whistle blew, I was almost sorry.

Except I needed to fish my phone out of its baggie and get back to work. Like, now.

Getting out of the kayak was every bit as graceless as getting into it. I could see how it would be far easier if you were willing to get your legs and feet wet, as Mr. Thetford could in his ugly waders.

Leigh and Olivia tried to angle for him to help us, but we got one of the concessionaires instead, and Mr. Thetford was too busy loading in the final class to do more than wave at us. I had one hour before the clambake required my attendance, and I made use of every possible second. Leigh and Olivia went on to their scheduled wetlands labs, and I went back to my picnic table.

But there was a slight difference in this conference call. I was feeling unusually good, so I took a moment to compliment my team before I unlimbered my plan. "Thanks for bearing with me," I said to the astonished silence through my headset. "You're doing a good job. This is hard, and I appreciate the time you're putting into it."

Finally, Jesse, the junior associate with the most time at the firm, gulped and thanked me. In for a penny, in for a pound, I decided.

"We'll all succeed or fail as a team," I told them. "We'll go faster when we coordinate our work and stroke together. When we win this case, I'll see what I can do about getting you all out of those cubicles."

Carla, the one whose cubicle was closest to my door and thus often the first one I called on when I needed something, uttered a yip of excitement.

Hmm. This was as much enthusiasm as they'd ever shown me. Lessons of the kayak. Or the wetlands. Or the bio teacher. Whatever. I laid out my plan and invited them to troubleshoot it with me. Could we help the witnesses emigrate permanently to a nation where taking their deposition would be vastly easier? We debated the merits and discussed the challenges. Once again, sixty minutes flew by.

The whistle blew again from the wetlands behind me, and by then, the smells from the catering truck were maddeningly delicious. "One-hour break," I told my team. "No, make it ninety minutes. Jesse, take everyone to lunch. Not too fancy. I'll expense it. Talk to you at two thirty sharp."

This time, the cheers were from more than one person. I left the call with a new sense of optimism.

This might work.

The school's lunch was delicious. Was it the food? The fresh air? My own hunger? I couldn't decide. I sat next to Leigh and her friends and discovered that I was grinning at their teasing and jokes.

"Mom!" Leigh cried happily. "What's happening to your mouth?" She giggled and pointed at me. "Are you smiling?"

Her teasing was wonderful. Her smiles had been in short supply lately, as mine had been, but I had to mask the fact that the teasing stung too. I never intended to turn into a woman who didn't smile, much less a mother who didn't. I spared a moment to curse my ex. Again. I was getting good at cursing West silently.

We'd been through a lot, my girl and I, and we deserved a few grins. I tickled her until she shouted with laughter. "Oh my god," I cried. "It's contagious! It's happening to you too! And now your friends!"

The four of us howled, falling off our Park Service log circle and pointing at each other. Neighbors got caught up in our hysteria, and soon it felt like the whole world was laughing and happy.

I could get used to this.

After lunch, Addie Belle, as chair of the field trip, gave a sweet, drawling little speech about how much fun the Jamaica Bay science class field trip was every year. Then she announced that Mr. Thetford would lead us in a sing-along. The boys clapped while the girls screamed their joy.

He'd taken off his waders. Now he was in a beat-up pair of cargo pants that did nothing to hide how nicely he was built. Apparently, I'd accused the jeans unjustly. The man just had a pretty backside. The choice of fabric didn't matter.

I resolutely put aside the question of how *no* fabric would look.

He pulled out an odd, sticklike instrument that he explained was a backpacker guitar, easy to travel with and almost impervious to harm. I wasn't expecting much, but the sound was surprisingly bright and pretty.

And Leigh was right. The man had a luscious, deep voice that was warmer than the bonfire. He began with the school song, which I didn't know at all and Leigh only knew a little. She took the occasion to lean over to me.

"Didn't I tell you?"

I nodded at her.

"Does he pass the audition?"

"I vote yes," I said emphatically. "You?"

She nodded happily.

"All right, it's unanimous. We have our first act for the talent show. Well done, talent scout!"

She grinned and laced her fingers with mine. I felt a burst of joy like sunshine.

Mr. Thetford led them in traditional songs (including chestnuts like "Michael Row the Boat Ashore"; the kids groaned, but the uncool nature of the song didn't stop them from singing along robustly) and modern hits (he could take requests, including Panic! At The Disco and Halsey, and the classes screamed happily through a rendition, astonishingly, of "Bohemian Rhapsody" that should have raised Freddie Mercury from the grave in amazement).

And then Addie Belle insisted, "You play one of yours, Bart."

He shrugged and swung into a song I was surprised to recognize. It took a moment before I got it. It was a bouncy, happy hit by a country band that had been big a few years back, "Alison's Tractor."

I looked around for someone to ask and saw the timid

woman who had pulled me into kayaking. "What did she mean, 'one of his'?" I asked.

"He wrote it. He's quite the songwriter, our Mr. Thetford," she said dreamily. Her hands splatted together as she clapped along with the chorus. "'Alison's tractor goes putt, putt, putt, she oughta be in school now, but, but, but . . . '"

It was silly. And undeniably catchy. He'd captured the joy of a young woman who just wanted to tend the family farm, and he made the whole world dance to her happiness.

I found I was dancing too.

It threw a whole new light on the bio teacher.

Interesting.

9

BART IN THE BACK SEAT

BART

Both of the Woodley twins forgot they were allergic to shellfish. How do you forget a thing like that?

They weren't in any danger. Terrence's throat swelled up a little and Trevor reported his fingers were tingling, but an allergic reaction was an allergic reaction. Emergency Protocol A was enacted. Addie Belle put them in her Escalade with their homeroom teacher (a sweet hippie chick I'd dated for a few indifferent weeks when I first started at Hamilton) and "Toodled" them all off to the emergency room.

This required some rearranging. Addie Belle had delivered the core staff to Jamaica Bay an hour before the kids arrived so we could set up. Now we needed rides home.

Bill Cavendish, from the school's main office, took over logistics. He didn't even blink when I pointed to Callie Lyndon's name for my ride home. I'd been hearing music in that woman's voice every time we came together. I wanted to know if it could continue.

Her daughter, Leigh, was thrilled. I was treating her very carefully. A young crush was nothing to laugh at, and I wanted her to feel safe and respected until she realized what an old has-been I am and moved on to someone her own age.

(He'd best treat her with respect, too, whoever he was. I was particularly fond of Leigh, and any future boyfriend might discover she had an old fart in her shadow, ready to rough up any punk who treated her poorly.)

I was getting possessive of Leigh and her family. Might have to watch that.

By the end of the day, both the seventh and eighth grades were exhausted. A little smelly, a little sunburned, plagued by sand in small crevices, but happy. As each car pulled out of the parking lot to head back to the school, I knew those rides would be a lot quieter than they had been on the way over.

The caterers had taken my kayak when they left after lunch, but I was still wearing my waders at the time. (I was on the deeper end of the seine net for the afternoon when the kids and I were assessing the life web in the marsh estuary, so I had the waders on to stay dry in cool, knee-deep, late-September water.) I had to load my stinky waders, regretfully, into the pristine trunk of Callie Lyndon's sensible Volvo.

I kept the backpacker guitar at hand. I had a song in me that I needed a few quiet minutes to explore, and I hoped she'd listen and maybe comment on it. Would the song resonate as strongly for the muse as it did for the musician?

Leigh volunteered to take the middle seat and was thus tucked up against my side on the ride home, with Shane beside her. Olivia rode shotgun, turned around backward so she didn't miss anything.

"Will you play something for us, Mr. Thetford?" Leigh asked.

"Do you mind?" I asked Callie when she caught my eye in the rearview.

"I'd like it," she said politely—and I heard the bridge to the flute song as she spoke.

Amazing. Years of hearing nothing, and now she suggested songs to me every time she opened her mouth.

Wait your turn, I said sternly to that silvery flute. *I've got a wetlands piece to percolate.*

"Okay. I've got something I'd like to work on, if you don't mind."

"You're writing a song right now?" Leigh was excited, and Shane squealed.

"It might not be very good," I apologized. All three girls shook their heads at me. They were thrilled to be audience to a creative process. We'd see.

I'd been itching to work out the notes and chords to fit the piece unspooling in my brain. It was Leigh who made the connection first.

"That's the curlew's call!" she said happily.

I grinned. It was such a thrill to be understood. "Good. That's what I was going for. Can you hear the wetlands? Listen. How does this sound? Do you like this?" I played a sleek passage meant to imply sunlight on water. "Or does it sound better like this?"

The variation was subtle, but they were happy to debate it, asking me to play them both again.

"What do you think?" I asked Leigh's mother.

She alternated between watching me in the mirror and the road ahead, navigating the traffic. "Is it the channel between the grasses? The—what do you call it? The water road?"

"It is," I said, not letting my excitement show. "You can hear it?"

"I hear it more in the first one."

"Me too," Leigh said.

Everyone agreed the first passage was the one to keep.

"All right," I said. "Here's what I'm thinking for the chorus. It's just a beginning, but see what you think of this."

I sang what I'd been hearing all afternoon, a strong, bold melody that played off the "water road" passage.

There are no wrong choices, but you have to
make a choice
Indecision is the killer
Sing out, I need to hear your voice
Courage.

Her mouth fell open at the first words, and Leigh and Olivia both shouted. Shane wanted to know what was going on.

"That's what my mom said in the kayak!" Leigh screamed. "Play it again!"

"I'm going to have that word *courage* repeat through the chorus," I explained. "Like a pulse, a slow drumbeat. Can you hear it?" I sang it again, this time knocking against the guitar in the rhythm that I heard the words. "It would sound better if this dinky little guitar had any resonance."

"Teach us," Leigh begged. "How does it go?"

"Okay. Listen."

We were stuck in the inevitable traffic going into the city, and the ride took every bit as long as I expected. By the end, they were all singing the drone of "Courage . . . courage . . . courage," as I laid the melody of the chorus over them.

It was pretty exciting for me to bring that song to life.

They seemed to like it too. "It's like the stroke of the kayak paddle," Callie said as she pulled into the school. "The courage beat—it's pulling us through the song."

I felt a burst of gratitude as she spoke. I hadn't made the connection, but she was right. You could definitely kayak to this song, and the paddle dipping into the water on either side would exactly match the beat I wanted. She'd seen it before I had.

I was beginning to have a problem when it came to Callie Lyndon. I was afraid I was starting to need her.

The girls had to check in with their homeroom teacher when we got back to school, and that left me alone with Callie for a moment, standing at the trunk of her car. I fished out my waders. "Thank you for the ride."

"It was nothing." She seemed to have trouble finding something to say. "Do you have far to go? Traffic is terrible."

"Not on my bike, it won't be," I said. She looked startled.

"Motorcycle?"

"Ten-speed."

"You're going to bike home? In the waders?" She was laughing at me, and I laughed too.

"I'll leave everything here. My buddy will come to pick up the kayak with me this weekend. I'll bring the guitar, though. I might have to pull over halfway there and work on the verses. I think I can hear the bridge to the song."

"You'll never get home." Her grin faded to a nice smile. "Do you have far to go?"

"I'm up in the Bronx."

"The Bronx?" She was startled. "You're going to bike to the Bronx after kayaking and seining the entire day? Don't be silly. Get back in the car. Leigh and I will give you a ride."

I backed away from her car. "No, really. I can't. Thank you, but no."

She cocked her head at me. "Why not?"

I couldn't dream up a socially acceptable lie. I had to tell her the truth. "Because you overwhelm me. I can't take it anymore. The ideas are piling up in my head." Her face fell in astonishment, and I stepped back toward her, impulsively taking her hand. "I hear music every damned time you speak, Callie."

Her hand clutched convulsively in mine. "No, you don't," she said with what sounded like a measure of desperation in her voice.

"I do," I insisted. "You're a muse, Callie. You're my muse."

"The hell I am!" she shot back, her reaction a slap to my face. She yanked her hand away. "I am not a muse! Leigh!" She turned from me and strode forward quickly, grabbing her daughter. "Come on, baby. Let's get home."

Leigh, bewildered, allowed herself to be dragged to the car. She waved to her friends and to me, and then they were gone.

What the hell had I said?

10

COFFEEHOUSE CONCERT

CALLIE

After that, I did what I should have been doing all along: I kept my head down. I got to work. I stopped expecting help until I had it in hand.

That plan was working for me too. I helped Cleo fill out an appeal to the city for an extension on the work deadline for Mimi's house. I organized the foolish talent show. And at work, Lawrence was impressed with my plan to help the witnesses emigrate so we could thoroughly depose them.

He helped me put together a review group—not uncommon in these overwhelming multinational cases. It was necessary to get buy-in from all the parties to ensure we weren't persuading the witnesses to take an action only to benefit our side of the case. For most meetings, I represented AresCorp and Hoare Ascutney, and Human Rights Watch sent their lawyers. (They were the ones who'd brought the case against AresCorp after the Syrian courts dismissed the charges.)

We had a JAG military lawyer and two deputy secretaries from the US State Department on hand. The judge on the case helped mediate on legal gray areas via online meetings or in the courthouse, but he never met with any one of us alone to avoid even the appearance of impropriety.

Then there were two lawyers who were supposed to be skilled in immigration law, hired by two of the witnesses in Syria, who'd expressed an interest in emigrating to Sweden. (As I reviewed the status of Syrian refugees around the world from Human Rights Watch, I agreed with their choice.) The lawyers were hopelessly outclassed, but the Human Rights Watch lawyers watched out for them.

We also pulled in diplomats from the Swedish embassy. They were very tall and unfailingly polite.

The third Syrian witness to the atrocity (I'm sorry—I meant to say "the event") was a nurse who had been bombed out of her hospitals no fewer than four times, at least three times by her own government because she'd insisted on treating rebels as well as government soldiers wounded in battle. She'd already snuck her family out of Syria, but she herself felt called to serve her neighbors and refused to leave. She offered her deposition through any impartial lawyer we could all agree on.

The situation was so dangerous, the only people who would dare go into Syria were either military, which would escalate the investigation in a way the State Department was terrified of, or the Human Rights Watch researchers, who were willing to risk their lives crossing the border illegally. Since they were my opposition, I was reluctant to accept that offer. We were still working it out.

I assigned my team of associates and interns one participant each. We held mock meetings before every real meeting so I would be completely prepared. The associates loved it. They became involved in each of the parties' motivations and goals, and I suspected we might lose Jesse to

Human Rights Watch; he was a little too impressed with their work. Huge cut in pay, but you'd go straight to heaven when you died.

(They might lose *me* to Human Rights Watch. Those guys are heroes. I'd deny it if questioned, of course.)

Lawrence headed any of the group conferences that involved the judge so he could handle the tricky politics of the legal world. Otherwise, he was confident enough in my abilities to let me handle the day-to-day work, he said, so I knew I was doing a good job.

And he hadn't put a hand on my knee since the first time, or made vague, insubstantial mentions of "our talk." I could almost forget he'd made a pass at me . . . if it wasn't for Addie Belle.

She was everywhere. Perched delicately in the law office's lobby, charming the receptionist. Coming out of the ladies' room as I was going in. Found watching me from the door to Lawrence's suite. I began to expect her to appear from my closet at home.

And of course, she was at Hamilton Academy, where I was spending far too much time on the talent show.

Each time I saw her, she gave me a sweet smile and her finger-waggling "Toodles!" call. I'd taken to raising a hand in salute and calling, "Ciao ciao!" in reply. Suitably continental, and the sound of the words reminded me of a big, fussy, overbearing dog.

A female dog.

But thinking of Addie Belle as a chow chow was small comfort when she insisted that I report to the school's board of directors every other week on my progress. "So we can help you if we see you getting in over your head, dear."

Right. So they could help me.

I retaliated by using my new State Department contacts

to strike up an email conversation with the wife of our new ambassador to Brunei.

Delilah Stratford had run the talent show for the past three years, and she proved to be a font of valuable information . . . until her emails suddenly dried up. My requests for assistance went unanswered, and I knew my own personal chow chow had cornered the ambassadress and shut her up.

That was fine. By that time, I'd already discovered not only how she'd broken the work up into seven committees (talent, facility, individual fundraising, corporate fundraising (!), hospitality, organization, and sales and marketing), but she had also sent me the names and emails of the former committee heads, four of whom were wondering why they hadn't been asked to help again this year and were ready to get to work.

The other three committees had been chaired by the parents of students who'd graduated or moved in the last year, but two of them gave me the names of parents who would probably be willing to help. The last committee—talent—remained unfilled, and I figured Leigh and I would have to sort that out ourselves.

Funny how Addie Belle, in all her discussions of what was expected, had failed to mention any of the people who might help. She looked as if she'd unwittingly sucked on a lemon when I outlined my helpers at the subsequent board meeting, and she was unable to withhold the names and donation amounts of last year's donors when I asked the board for that information.

So, I felt as if I was keeping my head above water. "Ciao ciao," I saluted her as I left the board meeting.

Above all things, I avoided the handsome bio teacher, cringingly aware that I'd ended our nascent friendship under the most awkward circumstances. I had enough to handle. I couldn't take on an artist's fragile ego.

Even if his "Courage" song did sometimes echo across my brain.

Courage, indeed.

I thought I'd slipped his net until Leigh cornered me one morning as I was about to leave for work.

"Mom!" Her tone told me this was A Big Topic.

"Leigh?"

"I've been good, haven't I? And my grades have been excellent. Mrs. Kim has given you good reports, right?" I nodded cautiously at each statement. "Well, Olivia, Shane, and I want you on Friday night. Can we have you?"

My schedule was blazoned on the inside of my eyelids. I knew it and lived it. But to stall, I made a show of consulting my calendar. "I should be free after seven on Friday. What are you thinking?"

"A night out. You and me and my friends." She saw me getting suspicious and added, in her direct style, "Don't make me play the absentee mother card. I'll do it if I have to."

I offered an unwilling snort of amusement. "All right. No absentee mother here. What are we doing?"

"There's a coffeehouse in Chelsea we want to go to."

The clock was ticking. I needed to get to work and the car service was waiting at the door, but this was too curious to miss.

"Why?"

"There's going to be a mini reunion for UVM graduates."

I felt like a dog trying to understand how his master's voice could be coming from the Victrola. Stating the blatantly obvious, I said "You're not a graduate of the University of Vermont."

"That's okay. Anyone can go. We want to hear the band they've got playing."

I lost interest. "Fine. Text me the address. I'll put it on my calendar."

"Thanks, Mom." She kissed my cheek. "Can you drop me off at school? It's cold out there."

"Are you ready now? All right, let's go."

The cold snap held for the rest of the week, and by Friday, the city was trapped beneath ominous gray clouds. A blizzard was heading for New York, and I took care to pack up everything I might need if I was forced by snow to work from home for the weekend.

All three girls were waiting in the apartment when I got home. They'd passed the afternoon dyeing Leigh's hair again. This time, it was a gleaming emerald that I found even more disconcerting than the turquoise, but the girls seemed pleased.

I dressed in old jeans and big lined boots and dismissed Mrs. Kim. "Go straight home, Mrs. Kim. The snow's already started." The girls rushed in excitement to the windows to coo at the thin flakes now sleeting down.

Mrs. Kim and I agreed that if the city got hit as hard as the forecasters predicted, I'd be working from home on Saturday, so she could have the day with her family. She scurried away, a broad grin on her face.

"You sure you want to go to your band?" I asked the girls. "It's going to be a pretty big storm."

They insisted they were desperate, so we loaded up with coats and hats and mittens and headed out for a brisk walk to Chelsea.

The coffee shop was a tiny storefront, but a steep staircase led down to a cavernous basement with a ring of tables and booths around a stage. The sign said, THIS

NIGHT ONLY: BUMP AND THE BOYS - THE TRIUMPHANT RETURN!"

"You want to see a band called Bump and the Boys?" I asked Leigh, but she and her friends just giggled.

The place was already packed with shouting, happy Vermont graduates gathered around a bar (I thought it was just a coffeehouse), and we looked in vain for a place where we could sit together.

I found a large booth in the back corner that held only a pretty Latina woman and a young boy. Throwing myself on her mercy, I asked if we could join her. She and the boy obligingly moved over, and we slid in.

"We should have gotten here earlier," I said.

"It wouldn't have mattered," the Latina woman said. "We got here with the band, and the place was packed. The reunion met here at two, I think."

"You're with the band?" Leigh asked interestedly. "Really?"

"I'm with Bump," she said, smiling. "Not the Boys. Well, this boy. This is Fonse. Short for Alfonso." She ruffled the head of the child next to her, who regarded the girls gravely.

"Your hair is very pretty," he said politely to all three of them. They cooed and declared that he was adorable.

"I'm Pandora," she went on, and we made our introductions. "How do you know the band?"

"One of the Boys is our bio teacher," Leigh said happily.

It was like a spike through my heart, but the conversation went on as if I hadn't winced. That was a man I didn't care to see again.

"Oh, you go to Hamilton Academy?"

"We do!" The conversation bubbled along easily, Fonse declaring that he was part of the Hamilton PrimaryNet to track the weather. Eventually, Leigh looked at me. She was startled to find me glaring.

"Why didn't you tell me?" I hissed.

"What? About Mr. Thetford? Oh. I guess I forgot."

Right. She forgot. So sure.

Fine. I'd figure it out. He probably wouldn't notice us in the back of the room anyway. I had my laptop in my shoulder bag. I pulled it out and apologized for checking my emails. Leigh rolled her eyes but recognized that at least I hadn't put in my earbuds.

I half monitored the conversation, which was cheerful and less moody than you'd expect from a twelve-year-old and two thirteen-year-olds with crushes on their teacher. Pandora and Fonse were interested in everything and seemed grateful for someone to talk to who wasn't busy drinking and reconnecting with old friends.

I began to relax, which was always a mistake.

Because of course, "Bump" of Bump and the Boys stopped by to say hi to his girlfriend before they went on, and of course, he brought the band with him.

"Hey!" Mr. Thetford said when he saw Leigh. "Look at that green hair! You were turquoise this afternoon in class, Leigh. That was fast! I'm going to have to rewrite some lyrics on the fly tonight! Thanks for coming—"

He'd noticed me.

My smile was prim and uninviting. He shivered as if cold and introduced his students to Bump (whose real name was Robert, but that was apparently never used). We were all in turn introduced to the other Boys, Ajay, Winston, and Saul.

"What do you mean, you'd have to rewrite lyrics?" Leigh asked eagerly.

He winked. He *winked*. I couldn't have been more annoyed. He had to have studied how cute that was in the mirror; the girls next to me melted from adolescent lust. “Stick around and see. We ready, Bump?”

They took the stage to thunderous applause from the Vermont alumni, and I saw a subtle transformation. Mr. Thetford looked . . . relaxed. He looked easy. He looked at home as he exchanged grins with his bandmates. It was as if a tension he always carried had vanished. Poof.

As soon as they started to play, I realized he’d dialed it way back on the field trip so he didn’t outsing the kids. Barton Thetford had a voice of extraordinary power and range. He’d definitely had training and had clearly taken care of his instrument.

And that wasn’t even considering the authority with which he handled his guitar, a showy, gaudy thing that put the backpacker to shame.

Bump was the band’s leader. He introduced the songs and cajoled the crowd from his microphone behind the drum kit. But there was no doubt that Bump’s lead singer had a star quality none of the others could match.

Wow.

I realized my mouth had fallen open. I closed it with a snap and looked around to gauge the effect on the girls.

Predictable. They were starry-eyed, all three of them.

Pandora caught my eye and nodded to the girls. It was too loud to speak, but we exchanged indulgent smiles. Her warmth said, *We were young once too* and my reply was, *I don’t think I was ever that young.*

On the one hand, I was happy Leigh was experiencing some fairly typical milestones for a tween’s life. She’d been buttoned-up and organized for so long. I was happy to see her acting her age—and the object of her longing was clearly a decent man who would handle her crush with dignity and kindness.

On the other hand, I could see my daughter falling into a pattern I knew and feared far too well. The women in my family were fatally attracted to handsome artists who treated us badly. That wasn't a future I would endure again, and it was one I wanted to keep her away from too.

I pushed down resolutely and forced to the ground any thought that my daughter and I were crushing on the same man. That would not do.

Their set mixed what I assumed were original compositions with covers of other artists (the crowd sang along with all of them, so clearly, the originals were from their school days). They did a far tighter cover of "Alison's Tractor" than the kids had done on the field trip, and it wasn't until then that I realized how good the entire band was—how well they gelled together.

Bump spoke after the vigorous applause for "Alison's Tractor."

"It's been a while since we had any new music to share," he said. "Want to hear what we've been working on lately?"

Yes, it appeared the crowd *did* want to hear that.

Bump rolled them into business with a pulsing cadence like a heartbeat. A funked groove that got the hips going. Winston's piano and Ajay's bass guitar slipped in and out, and Saul, on saxophone, embroidered a melody that seemed familiar. When Bart began to sing, I knew it was the song he'd written in my car.

The girls gasped and shrieked as he launched into the first verse.

At the fork, the gleam of turquoise
To left? To right? What dreams? What joys?
Which chances wait around the bend?
Which path is right? Where waits my friend?

The girls screamed their part of the chorus, adding that repeated "courage" along with Ajay and Bump on more official backing vocals. I found I was singing it too.

There are no wrong choices (Courage),
But you have to make a choice (Courage)
Indecision is the killer (Courage)
Sing out. I need to hear your voice
Courage.

Bart looked at the band for the second verse. He'd said he was making a change on the fly, and they were watching him to not miss it.

Your point of view is always changing
From skyscraper heights to water bug's ranging
And all the things you thought you knew
Can vanish in a flash of blue
And all the things you thought you'd seen
Can vanish in a flash of green

It was the two extra lines he'd added when Leigh had dyed her hair that they were improvising. They did a pretty good job of it too.

The bridge was instrumental, with Saul's saxophone duplicating the curlew's call. Then Bart repeated the first verse ("At the fork, a gleam of emerald / To left? To right? What joys?") and then he sang the chorus twice, building to a shouted close everyone sang along with.

Why was my throat so tight? Oh. Because I was screaming with the others, thrilled and uplifted and excited and proud as could be. He'd written that in *my* car.

The girls were almost hyperventilating, and Leigh's eyes

were huge. He'd written a song for her, and she was dying of excitement. Whatever else happened in her life, this was a single moment she would never forget.

Neither would I.

Bump told the wildly enthusiastic crowd that they were working on other new songs; they might have more for them at the next reunion. They only quieted the impatient crowd by returning with a song driven by pure rock energy. I could barely hear myself think.

But I could feel my heart beating.

11

NOVEMBER SNOWS

CALLIE

Leigh and her friends begged to stay after the band finished its set; they wanted to congratulate their teacher. My weather app (and the forecast of Fonse, our in-booth weatherman) made it clear that every Saturday morning activity would be canceled because of snow. I texted Shane and Olivia's parents for permission for them to stay out late. (Their sleeping bags were already on the floor of Leigh's bedroom, but I always figured informed consent was critical when I was accorded temporary parental oversight. They could have allowed their girls to spend the night without giving permission for an extended late-night coffeehouse visit.)

Both responded quickly. The snow was keeping everyone inside and near their phones. "We can stay," I reported.

The girls high-fived each other and Fonse cheered. He had managed to wriggle between them and was being taught by Shane how to braid Leigh and Olivia's hair together, strawberry red twining with sleek green. I avoided warning them against the tangles that might lock their two heads together. Everyone was having fun. What could possibly go wrong with that? (Ha! When disaster struck, I'd figure it out.)

"I'm glad you're staying. We're here until the bitter end. We came in the truck with Bump and Bart." Pandora's soft voice was much easier to hear now that the music system had gone back to piping the hits of a decade ago. The alumni had begun to move on to their next stop, a large, noisy bar two blocks over.

The band was packing up, using dollies to wheel the piano and various amplifiers backstage, to (I presumed) a waiting truck. All five of them were frequently stopped by admirers who came onstage to reminisce and congratulate them.

And then Bart was squeezing into the booth, one hand on a heavy guitar case. "Greetings, seventh-grade bio. What did you think?"

"And me!"

"Beg your pardon—greetings, seventh-grade bio and Fonse. Did you like it?"

The youth of America spoke over each other in their rush to praise Bart and the band, and then the booth got even more tightly squished as Bump slid in on the opposite side.

"All packed up?" Bart asked.

"Oh, sure. Tight as a tick. Unfortunately, that tick is stuck fast."

"What?" Pandora gasped.

"I thought you had snow tires on that thing," Bart said.

"I do. Lots of tread too. Won't do us any good. The alley

is plowed in solid. And the snowbank has been icing over and then getting snowed on for the last two hours. It's like cement. We're going to need jackhammers to break through."

The lights in the enormous basement flickered and then came back on. I put my hand on my phone—an excellent emergency light, should the power fail.

"How will we get home?" Pandora asked nervously, her hand reaching out to cradle Fonse's dark head. "I don't want to be trapped in a subway tunnel all night if there's a blackout."

"Don't worry, baby. I'll find us a hotel down here."

She shook her head. "In the middle of a blizzard? It'll cost every penny we have."

Leigh looked at me urgently. I saw no choice.

"If you can stand a crowd, Leigh and I would be glad to give you shelter. We're nine blocks down and one over, if you don't mind a walk in the snow."

Fonse was already bouncing in delight, and Bart, Bump, and Pandora were exchanging glances. Bump spoke for the group. "We'd be grateful. Thank you."

"Thank you, Callie," Bart echoed. Leigh, Shane, and Olivia were giggling and whispering, too excited to hear what the others were saying.

"Well, the accommodations won't be luxurious, but you can wait out the worst of the snow, and we've laid in supplies, so we'll have plenty to eat. What about the other guys in the band? Do they have someplace to go?"

Bump nodded. "They're joining the alumni on a pub crawl. God knows where they'll end up, but they're leaving of their own accord. We'll catch up with them later. Want me to put that in the truck?" He nodded at Bart's guitar.

"I got it," he said. "I'd rather not leave this behind—if you don't mind me bringing it," he added to me.

I couldn't think of a suitably casual phrase to explain how the very idea made me proud, so I just nodded. "Are we ready?" I asked. "I'd like to get these girls home before it gets too much later. And you, Fonse."

Everyone bundled up as best they could, and then I was the mama duck leading my ducklings single file through the snow to our nest. The city was eerily quiet. Occasionally, snowplows rumbled past and once in a while a police car, but other than that, the streets were empty.

The sodium-vapor lights were still shining—the power had flickered twice more, but each time it came back on—so we walked through a bright urban darkness, each snowflake spotlighted once it got within about twenty feet of the ground. Their path was quite a show, too, as the fierce winds were blowing and shifting rapidly.

The snow muffled all noise other than the wind, but occasionally I could hear Leigh and her friends talking excitedly. They had Fonse by the hands and were swinging him over curbs and snowbanks. The boy looked like he'd died and gone to heaven.

By the time we got to Twelfth Street, I was wishing I had one of those hideous, full-face, I'm-about-to-rob-the-convenience-store masks; my nose and cheeks were frozen. We piled into my small apartment—four adults, three teens, and a boy—and littered the living room with coats and hats and boots, set out to thaw and dry.

Hot chocolate was universally declared to be the only possible next step. (None of the adults wanted anything more serious. I was oddly pleased. There was a childlike innocence to snowstorms, I thought, and even coffee would have tainted that, much less stronger libations.)

I'd been planning distributions on the walk back. I had Shane and Olivia move their sleeping bags to my room, where they'd sleep with Leigh. I put Bump and Pandora in Leigh's double bed. (By this time, I'd grown fond enough of them both to mouth to Bump, *Don't have sex in my daughter's bed*, and he nodded gravely.) Bart got the sofa, and Fonse opted for the armchair as opposed to a nest on the floor in the bedroom with Bump and his mother; he was too excited with all the goings-on to want to miss anything.

"Where will you sleep, Callie?" Pandora asked me.

"With Leigh in my bed, but I've got work to do first. I'll take the kitchen so I don't disturb anybody."

Once she heard I was planning to work before sleeping, Pandora began hustling everyone into and out of bathrooms, distributing blankets and pillows with the efficiency of a drill sergeant. This was a woman I could get to like.

Leigh, Shane, and Olivia were persuaded to go to bed after exacting a promise that they could make waffles for everyone in the morning. We had to pry Fonse away to close the door on them. Once Bart lay down on the sofa, Fonse was willing to curl up in the big armchair. He was sound asleep long before the trio of girls stopped giggling in my bedroom.

Never mind. They could sleep as late as they wanted the next day.

Bump and Pandora thanked me again and withdrew. The apartment slowly settled into quiet, and I set up a mini workstation at the kitchen table, turning off most of the lights to make sure I didn't wake up Bart and Fonse in the next room.

The night had been exciting for me, too, but I settled down pretty quickly and managed to put in a few good hours on my case planning. Still, I must have been listening with one ear because I knew when Bart sat up and swung his feet to the ground.

He paddled on bare feet into the kitchen. "Am I disturbing you?" he whispered.

I shook my head. "Can I get you something?"

"Glass of water. I'll get it." He brought his glass to the table and asked with a look if he could join me.

I nodded. "I'm not keeping you awake?" I asked.

"Nah. I'm all keyed up from the gig." He grinned self-consciously. "Hard to turn off that high."

"I bet. That was something."

He lifted his jaw once in an acknowledging nod. "It felt . . . good."

"You looked comfortable up there." I regarded him critically. "Better than I've ever seen you. More relaxed, I guess." Honor-bound, I added, "Sort of like now."

He huffed a quiet laugh. "It's been a long time since I felt that good." He looked at my laptop. "I'm not disturbing you? I know you want to work."

In response, I closed the computer and found myself with the beginnings of a smile. "How long has it been?"

Thus invited, he slowly spooled out a tale. It must have felt safe in the half darkness, sitting in the neutral kitchen, to unburden himself, and I was a willing and fascinated audience.

He told me of his father's truck accident and of his sister's gruesome death by pancreatic cancer. Her name was Alison, which explained the origin of "Alison's Tractor." With almost-veiled pain, he told me of his mother Samantha, sitting alone and angry in a retirement community in Vermont, separated from her only son by her regret that he wouldn't take over the family farm that had meant so much to her.

Without thinking, I reached out and put my hand over his where it lay on the table between us. He dropped his head and wrapped his thumb around mine. "How long since you've seen her?"

"I visit a few times a year. She won't look at me. I think it's getting worse."

"And you stopped hearing music . . .?"

"When she sold the farm. When I disappointed her."

I bit my lip at the sorrow. "I might not have understood until tonight, but I know beyond the shadow of a doubt that you belong on a stage, Bart. You were meant to be a musician, not a dairy farmer."

He grimaced and leaned back, pulling his hand from under mine. "Yeah," he said as if he doubted it.

"It's been hard for you," I said uselessly.

He shrugged. "I guess I didn't realize how much I missed the music until I heard it again." He looked around the room, but he was seeing further than these four walls.

"You know, everyone here has someone," he said. "Bump has Panda and Fonse. Leigh's got her friends and you. You've got Leigh. I'm on my own."

I smiled. "You have Bump."

"Thanks." He grinned. "I don't know. Sometimes I feel so—"

He couldn't find the word, but I knew it. After the slow decay of my marriage and the bitter aftermath of a divorce, I knew the word well.

"Untethered," I said.

He looked up, eyes bright. "That's it exactly."

I nodded. "It's all on me. Who cares if I succeed or fail?"

His quick inhale surprised me. With an apology, he grabbed a loose paper on the table and fumbled for a pen.

"What?" I said.

He shook his head, scribbling.

"Did you just hear music? In *that*?"

"I hear music every time you speak, Callie," he said absently. "Would you mind if I got my guitar? I'll be quiet."

"Go ahead."

He was back in a moment, the fancy mother-of-pearl inlay on his guitar gleaming softly in the low light. "Keep working. I don't want to get in your way."

I opened my computer to appease him, but I was watching surreptitiously. His process was fascinating. He played, fingers on the fretboard, barely plucking the strings so the guitar made almost no sound, and wrote and played and scratched out what he'd written and played and grunted and played and sat in silence, listening to something I couldn't hear.

It took about forty-five minutes.

He looked up. "Want to hear it?"

Wordless, I nodded.

"The chorus is based on the first line of music I heard after an eternity of silence. That was when you accused me of having a nice ass."

"I did not!"

He grinned. "That's the way I heard it. Listen."

He began to play. The melody was haunting. This was no rocker. This was delicate and tender and sorrowful and bright, all at the same time. His fingers picked out notes that wove around his voice until I was lost in the sound.

Who cares if I succeed or fail?
It's all on me

Untethered

I used to be a part of something
One in a unity
I didn't know how rare that was
Until it was taken from me

Who cares if I succeed or fail?
It's all on me
Untethered

Now there's only me
I'm supposed to feel free
And I do. But lonely too
How could you leave me
Untethered?

I feel you where you used to be
How it was supposed to be
Everywhere I go, all that I do,
An empty spot right next to me
How could you leave me
Untethered?

Who cares if I succeed or fail?
It's all on me
Untethered

By the end, I was crying.

I cried for the failure of my marriage to West and for the loss of Susan, my former friend. I cried for Leigh and all I'd put her through. I cried for Mimi, my grandmother-by-choice, sitting in a beloved house that was decaying around her.

And I cried for Bart—for his dead father and dying sister and the mother who could not forgive her son.

"That's it," I said, my voice ragged. "You've captured it."

We both listened to the vast silence that followed his stunning, cathartic, amazing song.

12

IN THE BLIZZARD

BART

After a while, I realized I was sitting in her kitchen like a wiped-out zombie. I roused myself.

"Wow," I said mildly, which was about all I was capable of thinking. Then, without stopping to talk myself out of it, I reached over and took her hand. "I don't want to make you mad at me, Callie. Especially since there's a blizzard going on and you can't storm away." She offered the ghost of a smile, and I went on. "But that was all you, girl. That came out of you and through me, and I am—" I came to a halt, trying to sum up the emotions welling up in me. "I'm so damned grateful."

"Don't say it. Don't say I'm your—"

"I won't. But you are."

My muse. My fucking muse. My inspiration and my road back from silence and shame.

"Shut up." But she didn't mean it and I knew it, and we'd been looking at each other in the darkness for too long. I felt trembly, as if I was on the verge of making a fateful decision.

She opened her mouth, seeming not to know what she wanted to say. She was clearly surprised when she spoke. "This would devastate Leigh."

Shit. I'd forgotten all about Leigh—the trusting way Callie's twelve-year-old daughter looked at me, the shit she'd been through with her parents' divorce, the determination I felt that she'd get through her crush on me without getting hurt.

I let go of her hand like it was hot, sitting back again. "Right."

"How do you handle it?" she asked me. "You with your great butt." That made me chuckle. "All the girls must be crazy about you."

"Some of the boys too," I said with a smile. "It's a new day."

"Of course. What do you do?"

I nodded, thinking back to my sister's first crush on a boy who'd shredded her soul and to the great mentor who'd helped me when I was still a substitute teacher.

"I remember what an honor it is to be some girl's first crush. I treat her with dignity and respect—and distance—for as long as it takes for her to realize she deserves someone far better than me. I remain a person of benevolent authority. Sooner or later, I insist on homework or a school assignment that annoys them and they realize I'm more like their father than their Prince Charming, and they move on."

I was always relieved when they moved on—and a little saddened too. That made me a bad person, I guessed, someone with such low self-esteem that he'd miss the admiration of grade-school girls.

I frowned and confessed to that too. "And I try not to mind when it happens."

Why *not* unveil all my darkest character flaws? I'd already unloaded on the woman like she was a $300-an-hour therapist, and she hadn't run screaming. Yet.

"Does that include writing songs about them?" she asked me gently.

I looked up, surprised as hell. "'Courage' isn't about Leigh," I said. "It's about you, Callie."

"But . . . the hair color. Rewriting the lyrics."

"It's about you looking down the possible paths before you, always seeing your daughter's bright head in front of you, a pilot light to every choice, guiding your decisions. I'm sorry—does Leigh think—of course she does. Shit."

Callie's reaction was a blur of emotions. She looked like she was going to cry for her daughter, like she wanted to hug me, like she was going to shut herself into a closet and put her hands over her ears like a child.

She covered like a champ, though, and summoned a grin. "That's a forbidden word, teacher. Do you swear like that in front of your students?"

"Sometimes. They like it."

"You're going to get into trouble."

"Maybe. Don't you ever swear?"

"Not out loud."

"Go on."

"No, really. I'm a trial attorney, Bart." I loved hearing her say my name. "I can't be accidentally letting the f-bomb fly in front of a jury."

"F-bomb," I said. She was so cute. "Say it."

"No."

"Say it. Say *fuck*. There's no jury here."

"I'm not going to say it."

"Say it!"

"Do you think I'm a teenager succumbing to peer pressure?" She offered me an amused smile. I think we were both grateful the mood had shifted. We'd become playful, and she seemed relieved.

I was too.

"Oh, you'll say it," I threatened her. "I'm going to figure out a way."

"You can try."

"I know you *think* it sometimes," I said.

"Maybe. But I don't say it."

"Hmph." I looked at her, letting her see the challenge in my eyes. The moment drew to its natural conclusion, and I realized I felt restless. Twitchy. Like I had a ton of energy and nowhere to go with it. I would have liked to sing loud or done jumping jacks or something. "There are too many people in this apartment." I thought about it and knew I wanted out... and I wanted her beside me. So, I cobbled together a rough plan—my specialty. "Let's take a walk."

"It's—it's three in the morning."

"So? Don't you want to move around a little?"

She thought about it and gave a shiver, like she, too, was edgy. I saw the "what the hell" moment, although she probably would have said, *What the heck*.

"Okay. Let's go."

We were stepping softly around the living room, finding our respective foul-weather gear, when she stopped me. "Tell Bump and Pandora."

"They're asleep."

"Tell them anyway. I can't leave all these kids here without them knowing they're in charge."

"You're a belt-and-suspenders kind of girl, huh?"

"I am acting in loco parentis. A clear transfer of temporary parental authority is optimal," she said primly.

Oooh, lawyer talk. Sexy. "A-plus, Ms. Lyndon," I said. "As

an educator, I can certify that this is some prime-quality bullshit you spouted with such ease." I knocked quietly on the bedroom door and Bump appeared, tousled and sleepy. "We're going to take a walk. You're on deck for kid watch."

"There's a fucking blizzard going on out there, man."

"Yeah."

I turned away and Bump put out his hand to stop me. "The song is incredible, brother."

"You heard it?"

"We both did. Both of us lying here, crying like babies. Ever get tears rolling into your ears? It's a bitch."

The curl of a song drifted through my brain. Bouncy, up-tempo. Funny and sad too. Bump was a minor muse. It was nice to know Callie wasn't my only lifeline. I grinned at Bump and then swallowed, thinking of "Untethered." "I think it might be something."

"I think it might too. Go take your walk."

When we left the shelter of her building, I realized Bump was right. We were strolling into a nightmare of a storm. What could we have possibly been thinking?

More importantly, how was I going to keep this gorgeous woman next to me with all the weather gods viciously arrayed against us?

She needed a goal. That much was obvious. The woman was a planner.

"Maple syrup," I called to her from a foot and a half away, my words snatched by the shrieking wind.

"What?"

"Do you have maple syrup? Leigh, Shane, and Olivia are making waffles. You need maple syrup."

"I'll find something," she half shouted.

Another one I would have to school. I stopped and swung her to face me. "I am a son of the Green Mountain

State, for Christ's sake. I need maple syrup. And not that crappy Canadian stuff either. I need *Vermont* maple syrup. Preferably from the Northeast Kingdom."

By that time, it was twenty past three in the morning. We were standing on a deserted corner in lower Manhattan in the middle of a raging blizzard, and she was listening to me demand Vermont maple syrup without immediately abandoning me. I felt an irrational and overwhelming rush of infatuation.

"There's an all-night convenience store two blocks over," she said.

I felt a thrill like the adrenaline of victory. "Let's go."

We were stumbling down the second block when I realized my vision was getting blurry from more than the stinging snow. My own hot tears were leaching down my cheeks and icing over.

Too much had happened. The gig, the crowd's reaction to "Courage," sitting in her kitchen, finding "Untethered" like an already-cut-and-polished jewel waiting to be rescued from the silence.

Walking with her in the storm.

I was crying. Like a fucking idiot, I was quietly crying. And she knew it. She heard me sniff and called me on it.

"Are you crying?"

"It's the wind."

"It's not the wind," she said accusingly.

I looked up at the low clouds, willing myself to get it together. "I'm happy," I admitted.

I was lost. Utterly and hopelessly lost in a sense of absolute rightness, like a minor chord resolving to major at last. There was no use fighting it.

And then she wrapped her sensible, logical fingers

around my soul and spoke. "Is your nose too clogged to kiss me?"

I didn't know what reaction she expected—probably something more polite than she got. Without pausing for thought, I backed her into a windbreak next to the high stoop of the brownstone we were walking past. I cupped her warm cheek with my damnably thick gloves, and then I was unable to wait a moment longer. I found the overwhelming heat of her mouth with mine.

Down coats and insulated gloves kept us apart, but my heart was pounding in rapid staccato beats and I took advantage of her gasp to explore her mouth with my tongue. I was being greedy. I knew I needed to calm down, but I was helpless to resist.

Her breath and mine mingled, and I couldn't get enough of her. Through all the layers, I could feel her, her supple body and strength and heat reaching out to gather me in.

Her mouth, her tongue, even her teeth were delicious. I couldn't get enough and found I was gasping for air, for heat, for more of her. She seemed to be having the same problem, and I was suddenly overheating, burning up in my endless fucking layers.

But then the wind shifted again, throwing stinging snow onto our faces and down my neck. Sanity tried to make an appearance. She pulled back and I let her.

"Leigh," she gasped. "How can I do this to her?"

I leaned my forehead against hers, tugging her hood higher to protect her vulnerable skin. "All right," I said. "You're right. This is bad." We stood for a moment, feeling temptation like a magnet's pull, and then I resolutely stepped away. "Maple syrup," I said.

"Maple syrup," she agreed.

Down the street we walked again, very definitely not holding hands—I mean, gloves.

As I held the door to the convenience store for her, I looked at her in the lee of the wind and knew she was overwhelmed by the guilt of how this would affect her daughter. There had to be a way out. "You know, this is just a response to the creative force."

We stomped snow off our boots inside the door. "It is?" she asked.

"Yeah." I nodded to an implacable Korean man who, despite the storm, was hunched in his seat next to the cash register, reading his paper as if nothing unusual was going on. Pulling off my hat, I shook snow from my hair. "We're overwhelmed by it. That's all."

She shoved her gloves into her pockets and unzipped her coat. "Sure. That's all this is. Anyway, relationships don't last."

"Right. They burn out." We were in happy agreement.

"So, there's no need to tell Leigh anything." She was making perfect sense to me.

"It'll probably be burned out by tomorrow." I was filled with a sense of hope. Maybe I hadn't fucked up too badly.

"Absolutely. We won't be hurting her."

"Not a bit."

We moved around the store, looking for maple syrup in a shop designed to fulfill the yearning for cigarettes, lottery tickets, and a dubious salad bar. Staying apart from Callie was the mature, thoughtful decision and would safeguard a young girl's spirit. Why did I feel so bereft all of a sudden?

"Of course," she said thoughtfully, "It's not tomorrow *yet*."

I backed her against a case of energy drinks and buried my hands in her silky hair, cradling her skull. Immediately, the heat was back as I tipped her face to mine. I inhaled her, her kiss filling me with a spiral of excitement.

Thank god she'd unzipped her coat. Thank god I could press against her, feel more of her. It would have killed me if I hadn't been able to feel her breasts and stomach against me. The need for her touch was almost unendurable.

She arched her back, and I didn't even think of how bold it was—I put one hand to her waist and ran it up her torso. She mewled softly into my mouth when I cupped her breast at last, and I couldn't hold back my own groan of raw lust. It had taken an eternity to get to this point—an endless, torturous eternity—but now, at last, I was exactly where I needed to be. Cymbals fired in my head and I heard a pounding bass line, urging me on. A raw, passionate anthem was waiting to be explored. *Needed* to be explored.

"Hey," came the voice of the shopkeeper. "What the hell's the matter with you? This is a decent store. Get out of here with that."

Not even a word when two frozen refugees from the storm stumbled in, and *now* he was making his presence felt?

Callie and I parted, overwhelmed. I found I was slightly ashamed by how quickly we'd lost control—and absurdly proud too. I took her hand, her bare palm against mine like delicious, intimate sin, and we continued our prowl through the store.

And then I saw them.

"Look," I said, astonished. Four tins of maple syrup were snugged in between boxes of instant oatmeal and packages of dehydrated soup. I flipped one of the tins over and smiled at the label I found.

"I'll be damned," I said. "St. Johnsbury."

"Is that good?"

"Baby, it's the gold standard. Come on, let's get out of here."

I suspected I would have a long, uncomfortable night alone on the sofa in an apartment crowded with people I had no interest in sleeping with—most of them, anyway. Good thing dawn was on its way.

13

SOCIAL NOSHING

CALLIE

Leigh, Shane, and Olivia were more eager to wake up than I was. I buried my head in the pillows, glad to let them use my bathroom first. Interesting how deeply one can sleep after a toe-curling makeout session in a blizzard with a hunky musical genius.

The girls thundered through the room on their way to culinary-waffle brilliance in the kitchen. The sheer joy I could hear in my daughter's laughter was reminder enough of why I definitely could not speculate on how it would be to wake up in my bed with said hunky genius. My friend Rita, who was prone to picking up guys at truck stops and biker bars and then abandoning them once they wanted something more long-term, would tell me to sleep with Bart and move on, but life wasn't that elemental for me. An imaginary version of Cleo nodded at me in agreement. *Back off*, she would have said. *Don't hurt Leigh.*

For a while, I lay still, listening to the lack of city noise. The snow was still sleeting down, and urban life had temporarily ground to a halt. We were lucky to still have power.

Victory: there was one lone clean towel in the bathroom. A hot shower helped restore me to life. I came out my bedroom door, ready to face whatever waited, when the door to the bathroom down the hall opened.

It was Bart, coming out after his own morning ablutions. The T-shirt he'd been wearing under a plaid shirt was in his hand; the plaid had been upgraded to skin contact. (Distantly, I found I envied the shirt.)

His long hair was wet and slicked back, his feet bare. He saw me and stopped, an uncertain smile on his mouth.

"My daughter is going to love that look." I gestured with my chin, taking him in.

"What?" He patted his chest, his waist, making sure he was buttoned up.

"You look—I don't know. Wet hair, bare feet. It's intimate. Personal. Se—" I cut myself off before I could say *sexy*.

"And the jeans. Sorry. I didn't realize she'd be coming to the show. I know they're verboten," he said with a grin.

"Yeah," I admitted. "Turns out it wasn't the jeans. You just have a pretty butt."

His grin got bigger. "You think I have a nice ass."

I shook my head in mock despair, the ten feet between us seeming an impossible distance.

"Go ahead. I want to hear you say it. Say I have a nice ass."

"You *are* an ass."

"Ha! You said it!"

"Check your definitions, counselor. Referring to you as a donkey or burro is not considered profane. Words can have multiple meanings and be used and judiciously applied accordingly."

"I see. You'd call someone a bastard only if they were born out of wedlock."

"I'd call them illegitimate, although I doubt I would refer to it at all if it wasn't germane to the discussion."

"Man, you talk pretty."

Leigh rounded the corner in a rush, paying no attention at all to me. Lost in her view of her handsome bio teacher in a nonprofessorial capacity, she gaped and then spoke. "Waffles are ready, Bart. Come on!"

"Leigh," I chided her.

"What?"

"I think you call him Mr. Thetford, don't you?"

"Bump said we're all on a first-name basis for the duration of the blizzard. Is that not okay?"

"If Mr.—" I blanked on Bump's last name and looked to Bart for the assist.

"Weston," he offered.

"If Mr. Weston doesn't mind being called Bump, I'm fine with that, but he's not your teacher. You need to maintain a respectful distance with your educator." Christ, I sounded like such a stick in the mud.

"How about a compromise, counselor?" Bart grinned at Leigh. "What about Bart until noon and Mr. Thetford after that until the end of the school year?"

"And then back to Bart?" she asked hopefully.

"Depends on if you get me for chemistry next year. Speaking of chemistry, what molecular conversions are happening in your kitchen? Smells awesome." He tipped me a wink and allowed himself to be escorted to the smallest room in the apartment—so naturally, it was filled with all the people.

"Here, Mom. I saved your place at the table." Leigh had

put my laptop in my customary place and forced Bump into the corner.

Touched, I grinned at her first and then at him. "Do you mind being wedged in there?"

"I do what I'm told." Bump shrugged. "I'm useless in here. I'd go out and chop you some wood, but the city might object to losing their trees."

"Thanks anyway," I said. Pandora and the three girls were moving efficiently around the kitchen. Once again, she'd drill sergeant'ed them into tidy order.

"Pandora's a chef," Leigh announced. "She's teaching us to make brioche."

"I'm a cook, baby. Just a cook. But I can show you a few things."

From his perch on the counter, Fonse was directing the operations, a mixing spoon held up as his baton. "Our brioche is braided," he announced. "I now know how to braid. My brioche will be the best."

Bart and I found our seats at the table with the large form of Bump between us and settled in to watch the orchestration.

"What's on your work schedule today, Mom?" Leigh asked me. "The case?"

"Not today," I said. "I'm behind on the talent show. We need to put our heads together." I looked at Bart with new curiosity. "Hey. Help us with the talent, will you?"

He looked interested. "I heard you were taking that on. I'd be happy to help. What's your plan so far?"

It may have been the relaxed, happy mood or the forced intimacy of the snowstorm, but we managed to have one of the most productive meetings for the talent show I'd experienced yet. Besides suggesting various students and teachers to recruit for their talents, Bart had thoughts on luring in the more famous parents or former parents to show off their arts.

"That would help marketing," I said. "If we could say Basc Newton would do a stand-up act or Sheree would sing, we might have to find a different venue. People would come out of the woodwork."

Bump offered to put together a house band. I signed him up on the spot. Pandora ("Call me Panda, like they do," with a nod at Bump and his lone remaining Boy) wondered why we weren't having a catered opening reception.

"For high-dollar donors," I agreed. "That's a brilliant idea. Exclusive. Give a thousand dollars or more and come to a cocktail party with Basc Newton or Sheree."

"Basc Newton *and* Sheree," Olivia corrected. "We need to get them both to agree. My dad knows Sheree. At least, he says he does."

Bart was impressed with the idea of Leigh's video submission. "Why not open the talent show to other nontraditional offerings? Like . . . how about if the fifth grade did an art show on one theme or another? We could film their work and get the kids to do the narration. Produce a sweet reminder of childhood. Nudge some people into coughing up a donation."

"I love it." I made the note. "I was thinking about that. Let's make every person who comes to the talent show register their phone with us. Instead of waiting till the end to donate with a volunteer at a card reader, they can donate through their phones while they're sitting in the audience."

"You could make it a competition. Which act inspires the biggest donations?" Bump said. "A prize for the winner at the end, so every parent would have to pony up for their own kid's act."

"Smart. How do we praise the ones who give to shame those who don't?" Panda asked.

"I am liking the way you all think!" We brainstormed through the morning, sticky fingers coated with maple syrup. ("Hey," Bump said happily, "real Vermont maple. You're okay, Callie.") Buttery brioche crumbs were scattered between half-full cups of coffee and hot chocolate and fiendish plots and laughter.

I offered my idea of selling corporate sponsorships for the group's critique. The ad hoc talent show committee approved it resoundingly.

"Mom, how much do you have to make, again?"

"Last year, they made $1.06 million." There were indrawn breaths and shaken heads. "That would be enough to expand the Hamilton PrimaryNet to five other schools in the state. I think we can beat it. It won't be easy, but we've got some good ideas here. Sheree alone would lift us to an entirely new level, if that works out."

I was feeling better about the talent show than I had since the beginning. We were shaping the event into something special, and I felt like I might be getting the upper hand over Addie Belle. I didn't burden the others with her looming presence. It was enough that I knew she was there. I could handle her. I would figure it out.

The snow tapered off at about eleven, and Bump and Bart left to see if they could excavate the truck. Panda organized the kitchen cleanup squad. "Sit there and make your notes, Callie. We've got this. It's the least we can do to thank you for putting us up in the storm."

Yes, this was a woman I could come to truly appreciate.

She was talking with the girls about setting up informal cooking lessons at the deli where she worked when Bart appeared again. "Truck's out of the alley. Bump's double-parked out front and those plows are going to drive him off the road if we don't hurry. Ready to head home?"

While Panda and Fonse geared up for their journey in the snow, Bart threw himself casually into the chair next to me and picked up my phone. "Unlock this a minute, will you?"

I did, and he flipped to the texting app. Typing quickly, he sent a text and his phone beeped. He handed me my phone and pulled out his. Soon I saw a message on my screen as if I'd written it, plus the reply.

Now you have my number.

And I have yours.

He grinned at me and got to his feet again. "Thank you, Callie and Leigh. Thank you, Olivia and Shane. This has been the best rescue I've ever been a part of." The girls were delighted to respond, but he pointed sternly to his watch. "The witching hour has come. It's past noon. I'm your bio teacher once more. How do you address me?"

They giggled and called him Mr. Thetford.

He bowed formally from the waist. "It's been a dream. We gotta go." He whooshed Panda and Fonse out the door, and then the apartment seemed hugely empty for the four of us who were left, rattling around and mildly depressed by his departure.

"Oh my gawwwwwd," Leigh cried as she pivoted into the couch where he'd slept the night before. "That was awesome!"

They settled in to analyze every moment and word. I thought better of joining in to gush (much as I might want to) and put my earbuds in. Time for me to focus.

That evening, Olivia's entire family appeared, having

dredged up a dusty toboggan. They gathered Leigh and Shane into their large, happy mix and went off to the park to freeze and shriek and throw snow and generally have a snow-day kind of time.

In silence at last, I looked at my phone for a long time. Then I surrendered.

I hope she gets over you soon.

His response was quick. Was he staring at his phone, too, thinking about the night before?

In her time, not ours.

That was a good answer, but it also sort of annoyed me. Fortunately, the next text pinged in pretty quickly.

But I hope that, too.

I'd had time to calm down and remember that I'd sworn off men after the divorce from West. Bart was heating up that cooling-off time, and it was worth it to remember that he was the artist type I was drawn to, with disastrous results. Could I head off possible complications?

Tell me the truth: Do you have a girlfriend?

Or a wife?

I've been dating casually.

No expectations. No possible hurt feelings.
No wife.

I'm pretty sure I don't date casually.

I'm pretty sure you don't either.

I'm good with that.

Not that we're dating.

Right.

Just to put it out there.

Of course.

Well…

Well…

I wish we were dating.

Shh.

Sorry.

Night.

Night.

By Monday, I'd set up meetings with Bunky MacDonald, my individual fundraising chair for the talent show, and Nancye Kelleher, the chair of corporate fundraising. Both were alarmed but intrigued by the changes I was pushing. Bunky took on finding a phone app for immediate dollar contributions during the event, and Nancye asked for time to come up with some prospects for corporate sponsors.

I had almost two weeks before the next report to Addie Belle and the board and was feeling pretty good about the smart talent show fundraising I would be able to drop on them.

Nancye emailed me two days later to ask for times when she could set up a lunch with me to meet with some potential sponsors. The woman was on the job! I pushed her to move fast to have the sponsors in hand when I reported to the board. The night before the luncheon at a posh restaurant near the Metropolitan, I convened my Style Council by FaceTime.

Forewarned, Cleo had gone to visit Mimi so we could get our "grandmother's" opinion. Despite living in the most genteel poverty, Mimi had rubbed shoulders with society at a far higher level than any of us, and I considered her opinions to be invaluable. And Rita was in a truck stop in Denver, watching the fashion show with evident delight.

I showed them my favorite corporate suits. "This one in plum—don't you think this would inspire confidence in me?"

Leigh, cross-legged on my bed and in charge of holding the phone, called out her protest, and the others chimed in. It was Mimi's voice that eventually predominated.

"Darling," she said. "You're not going into this meeting as a shark. You're not a lawyer. You're a mother. Your look must be softer. And wealthier."

I eyed my closet with distrust. "Wealthier?"

"How about sexier?" Rita added. "You know—slinky. You could be the wicked divorcée."

"Stop!" Cleo laughed. "We don't want everyone thinking Callie is coming for their husbands! What about a long sweater over a skirt?"

I had both things. "Pencil skirt or flared?"

"Not a skirt," Mimi said firmly. "This isn't a movie. If you're going with a tunic sweater, you need leggings and boots. And your sweater should be chosen for the luxury of its content. Now, what do you have?"

By good fortune, my mother had given me an apricot

cashmere sweater that would go nicely with black leggings and black boots that I could hope looked expensive.

"One statement necklace and you're done," Mimi pronounced. "Leigh, you do your mother's makeup before you go to school tomorrow."

Leigh nodded, as obedient to Mimi as we all were.

"I can do it," I protested.

"No, you only know how to do 'corporate shark.' Leigh, we want soft and feminine. A no-makeup look. You know what I mean?"

"I can do it." Leigh was pleased to have a role other than camera operator.

"You will be beautiful and not at all aggressive, and they will love you." Mimi saw me through the eyes of love, and I basked in her generous opinion of me.

And it all went as planned. The next day, Leigh did my makeup with a surprisingly light touch, and I worked from home for the morning (so as to not terrify my team with nonlawyerly apparel). Then I set out to meet Nancye and her lineup of sponsors.

I spared a thought as I entered the restaurant ("I wish I had my corporate armor on"), but it was a momentary lapse. I threw my head back and prepared to sparkle.

The lunch was, I thought, a guarded success. Nancye and her four wealthy prospects (three men and a woman who was simply dripping in pearls) joined in happily to exclaim over the value of a STEM program like PrimaryNet to schools without Hamilton's resources, and, of course, to explore the possibilities for sponsorship name recognition. I was getting a $25,000 sponsorship vibe from a Bank of America vice president and an unspecific but positive feeling from the rep for the MacKenzie Foundation when I heard a sound that curdled my blood.

From behind me, it came—from deeper in the restaurant. "Toodles!"

I looked up. Heading for the door was Addie Belle McCrillis, a Christmas-themed Hermès scarf tied festively around her head in a bohemian style no one else had dared to wear since the Dior peasant look in the 1970s. She looked stunning.

She affected such surprise when she saw us that I knew immediately she'd not only been watching our entire lunch but also that she'd set it up from the beginning.

"Callie, darlin'!" she drawled. She waved at me with exaggerated movements, her phone clutched in her hand. "And Nancye! And—why, Bill Clarke! It's been an age!"

Of course she knew every person at the table. I was now pretty sure she'd arranged the entire party, had probably told Nancye where to seat everyone. But I didn't realize how deeply I was in it until she turned to the man on my left—Harry Someone, who ran a large family trust and looked vaguely familiar. I'd seen him on TV at some point but hadn't been able to place him.

"And Judge Naughton! Funny seeing you out and about! How are you?"

They chattered happily while I froze to my seat.

Judge Naughton.

Judge Henry Naughton.

The same Judge Naughton who was sitting on the AresCorp case.

The same man who wouldn't meet with us alone to avoid any evidence of collusion or improper behavior, the man who—yes, I'd seen on a TV screen. I'd seen him in his chambers and on the boardroom video monitor during his Zoom calls.

And I'd been sitting next to him, in the lawyer's-world

equivalent of civilian attire, in soft and feminine makeup. I'd put my hand on his arm and laughed at his jokes. And Addie Belle and her phone had been behind me the whole time.

She knew she'd gotten me. But that wasn't enough. Addie Belle didn't fight fair. She believed in kicking an opponent when she was down.

"Now, let's get a photo of all of you. Won't this be fun in the next *Hamilton Bulletin*? Scoot closer, Callie."

She jostled us all together—me, of course, squeezed to the judge's side with his arm around me—and took her photo, immortalizing my frozen grimace for all time. Then she expressed shock at the lateness of the hour and turned to leave.

Smiling sweetly, she raised her hand in a salute. "Ciao ciao," she said to me.

Then she was gone.

The others chattered easily, exchanging fun Addie Belle stories while I sat paralyzed. Before they could notice my woodenness, I pretended I'd gotten a call on my cell phone and excused myself.

Addie Belle was waiting for me patiently by the coat check.

"I've already sent the photos to myself," she said flatly, "so stealing or breaking the phone won't do you a bit of good. And I must say, I have some wonderful shots. My, you do photograph well." She pushed into my space, grinning up at me. "These are enough so the judge would have to recuse himself, and you'd have to start all over again. Well, not you. You'd be thrown off the case immediately." She savored her last words. "You'll lose your position. Publicly and with great shame."

I inhaled. She was absolutely right.

"Sweetheart," she said to me, "your corporate sponsorship idea is a good one. I'm going to land all those sponsors for you, and the talent show is going to meet its fundraising total. My decision to put you in charge is going to be seen as a great triumph for me." She regarded me critically. "You've seen my stick. Now, here's my carrot. You win that case for Lawrence—you make my husband look good—and I'll see that you get a job anywhere in the world you want. Anywhere, as long as it's not New York City. You can make a fresh start for you and that trashy, green-haired daughter of yours. Go after some other woman's husband." She'd lost some of the southern drawl as she sneered. "But either way, win the case or lose, once it's decided, you're quitting and moving on. Boston, Los Angeles, London, home to that backwater you flushed out of, I don't care. But you're gone. Do you understand me?"

I shook my head in shock and then nodded.

"You go near my husband—you breathe even a word of this to him or anyone else—and I use these photos. Darlin', is there any possibility you don't understand just how serious I am about this?"

"No," I whispered.

"Good. You're not the first woman I've peeled off my husband. Some of them weren't as pretty at the end as they were at the beginning. Don't underestimate my determination, Callie."

"I understand perfectly, Addie Belle."

"Fine. Then we're done here." The attendant had her adorable mink jacket. She took it with a sweet smile and left him a twenty-dollar tip. "Toodles!" she called—whether to me or the attendant, I could not say.

14

WEATHERING THE CHILL

BART

I couldn't get Callie to talk to me.

I knew we hadn't made any definite plans, but I'd assumed we were waiting for Leigh to grow out of the crush she'd had on me before Callie and I reignited the powerful heat between us.

That wasn't, apparently, how Callie saw it.

She wouldn't answer any of my texts. I tried calling and emailing her, but she'd only respond if I had a question about Leigh's education or the talent show.

We held three rounds of talent show auditions. The school's tradition was to pick the participants before the holiday break, so everyone had plenty of time to work on their act before the performance in March.

I'd been officially deputized to the talent committee in the golden week or so before Callie cooled on me, and Leigh was the only student on any of the committees. She and I and Callie comprised the entire talent subgroup. Leigh sat between her mother and me as we watched first every student audition (or explain a nontraditional entry, like a video), and then the teachers, and lastly, the parents.

The hugely popular stand-up Bascomb Newton had agreed to do a special set, promising both to cut the profanity from his act and also to focus his set on his son's time at Hamilton.

And Olivia's father did, it turned out, have the phone number for Sheree's personal assistant. In a stroke of amazing luck, the chanteuse had the evening off and was willing to sing two songs if we gave her the closing act spot. We were definitely willing. Having an artist like Sheree perform would lift this event into the stratosphere.

With those two celebrities locked in, some rising stars decided they wouldn't mind being seen either. We had a Broadway choreographer who agreed to bring a small dance troupe and a Lincoln Center second violin who offered a blistering "Flight of the Bumblebee."

Callie negotiated with the board to move the venue from the Hamilton Academy auditorium to a three-thousand-seat theater a few blocks away. Her marketing team began an aggressive campaign to sell tickets. Even three months out, ticket sales were impressive.

Things were going well.

Except that she wouldn't look at me. She would only talk to me if others were present. She never called me Bart.

I felt like a twelve-year-old with a crush on his bio teacher.

This was the depth to which I sank: I began to eavesdrop on Leigh and her friends.

Of course they were excited about the Christmas holidays. All it took was a fairly boring lab on osmosis to learn that Leigh was spending her break with her father in Washington, DC, and that Callie was taking her down on the train the day after school got out.

So, I bided my time.

I was at school that Saturday. With all the kids gone, it was a great time to get organized for next year without distractions.

And it left me free to text.

Callie.

Come on, Callie. Talk to me.

Maybe she didn't have her phone. Maybe she'd turned it off. Maybe she was in the Silent Car and hadn't heard my text ping in.

Right. Like the high-powered lawyer would ever be separated from her phone or team for even a moment. She was ignoring me. Time to drop a truth bomb on her.

You forced me to eavesdrop on seventh graders.

I know you're on a train.

Are you heading south still? Or are you coming back north?

With a burst of adrenaline that shot heat through my ears, I saw the three bubbles that meant she was typing a reply.

North.

So there's a big empty place beside you.

Huge.

Did you see your ex?

My ex and an ex-friend. I wouldn't leave her with him if "Cayenne" wasn't there, so that was weird.

Cayenne?!

Don't ask. Used to be Susan.

You hate her but you trust her too?

She loves Leigh. She won't forget Leigh is around.

And Leigh can call Cleo or Mimi if things get bad.

So that's good. How'd Leigh do?

Made me want to cry. She so badly wanted everything to be nice.

Wanted us all to be happy.

Hard on her.

On everyone.

Are you crying?

Shut up.

What time do you get to Penn Station?

Bart.

What? You need dinner, don't you?

Do you really want to go back to that empty apartment right away?

This is like emotional blackmail.

I'm weak and sad. Don't make this hard.

No obligations. Just dinner. Someplace easy.

I miss you.

Shut up.

I miss you, too.

I like that your grammar is so good in texts.

I am highly educated. I can't turn that off, you know.

Hey. I'm a teacher. I like it.

What time?

Callie?

6:41

Meet you under the big arrivals board.

I could see from the icon that she was typing, and then she stopped. Then she typed some more. Then she stopped. It took forever. Finally, her text arrived.

Just dinner?

Just dinner.

See you there.

I wished I was smart enough to have an ulterior plan—that getting her to eat dinner was part of my masterful scheme. It wasn't. I only wanted to see her. Talk to her. Make sure she was okay.

It took forever for the clock to tick over. I was wandering around smelly, crowded old Penn Station for an hour before her train got in, comparing the offerings of various delis and wandering down tunnels to strange commuter lines.

She looked so miserable when she arrived up the escalator that my decision to be calm and friendly melted. Instinctively, I scooped her up and hugged her.

After a startled moment, she hugged me back and began to cry.

"I'm sorry," she said. "I'm really not that upset. It's just that—"

She couldn't finish, and I held on while she dampened the shoulder of my jacket.

I edged her out of the crowd to a quiet space by the wall, tucking her shoulder bag (computer, I thought, so she could work on the train) between our feet with my backpack.

I was struggling with a crashing wave of possessiveness, drowning in a shattering urge to protect her. I wished there was a dragon I could slay for her, but her beasts weren't so easily confronted. That was frustrating for me. Plus, clearly, this was not a woman who responded well to a clingy male. I needed to pull myself together, even if I gained control a nanosecond before she did.

My dad had taught me to always carry both a pocketknife and a clean handkerchief. I'd swapped his old-fashioned square for a series of bandannas, but I'd seldom been as pleased with his advice as I was then, when I could hand Callie something to wipe her eyes and blow her nose once she stopped leaking.

She pocketed the bandanna firmly, promising to wash it and get it back to me.

Fine with me. Meant she'd have to talk to me again.

She took a deep breath and stood away from me, to my regret.

"I'm a wreck," she said. "I'm so sorry."

"You're a wreck," I agreed so we wouldn't have to dance through a round of *no you're not/yes I am*. "You need some food and a glass of wine. Can you handle a little walk? I know a good place."

She nodded as if her head was thick and clogged, which I was sure it was. "I'd love a little walk."

I had her shoulder bag with my backpack. It made me feel ridiculously happy, like she was letting me carry her books home from school. We collected my bike from the rack outside. She seemed more comfortable once I was walking it along between us. Her shoulders came down from around her ears, and after a few blocks, her stride got easier.

Even if she didn't realize why consciously, I knew the logic that was making her feel better. I had my bike. I lived in the Bronx. If I was planning on getting her into bed, I wouldn't have the bike with me. This really was just dinner. She didn't have to be on alert for Unwanted Advances.

By the time we got to the ancient Albert Tavern, the cold wind had picked a cherry flush out of her pale cheeks. The crease on her brow had eased. She was swinging her gloved hands at her sides instead of thrusting them protectively into her coat pockets. She looked better.

There was a fireplace on the second floor of the tavern that they still lit on chilly nights, and the upstairs was quieter than the main level. I put her in a booth in the corner and sat across from her. That way, she had more space, which meant fewer expectations. I saw her take a deep breath and then relax.

"Thank you. You're right. I don't want to go back to the apartment yet. It's going to be so empty."

"Sure. Wine? Something harder?" I looked at her critically. "They have a great hot cider."

"Cider," she said with relief.

This was a woman so profoundly on the defensive that I thought she might deck any knight errant who attempted to slay her dragons.

I talked her out of a salad and into a bowl of stew with fresh, hot bread. I sat across from her and talked about the talent show and Leigh's intelligence and why a dairy farmer is inclined to turn up his nose at mass-produced cheese.

All the while I watched her, drank her in, teased apart the dozens of melodies that were floating in my head. Maybe it was the three silent years of depravation, but I hadn't felt so filled with music since I was a kid. On the outside, I was grounded and calm and casual. Inside, I was floating about four feet off the floor with a tickle in my belly, like the hanging moment before a roller coaster goes over the first drop.

She sat back contentedly. She'd felt comfortable enough to order a glass of wine with her meal, and she held the half-full glass.

"I guess I owe you an explanation, Bart."

I raised an eyebrow. "For what?"

She winced. "For the muse thing."

Ah. A prickly topic. She'd reacted so strongly the one time I'd called her a muse, I'd never dared bring up the word again. "Okay."

She looked around the room, the firelight playing lovingly over her face. "My ex is—" She stopped. "When I got married—" That, too, was apparently the wrong beginning.

She took a large gulp of wine, sat forward, and produced an emotionless recitation as if making a summation to a jury.

"I was seventeen when I met West. I was in my first year of college. He was teaching art and needed models for his drawing classes. I got pregnant with Leigh, and we married before I was eighteen. West is quite a brilliant sculptor."

"Hang on." Something was tickling at my memory. "Wait. West. As in Westmore Peacham?"

She nodded with a resigned look on her face.

I worked it out. "There's a Westmore Peacham sculpture at Pier 66. I've always loved it. It's called *Wood Nymph*, even though it's made of steel—"

I envisioned the statue, fully fifty feet tall, of a graceful young nude who gazed out across the Hudson to freedom (if Weehawken could ever be considered freedom). And then I realized why the statue looked so familiar.

"And you sure are pretty without your clothes on, Callie."

"Yeah. That's me. He said I was his muse."

The words were complimentary. The delivery was pure pain.

"And that was a bad thing?"

She shrugged, uncomfortable. "It's a bad pattern for the women in my family. We fall for handsome artists who do us wrong. My father had a thing for muses too. I don't like to admit it, but Callie is short for Calliope, the Greek muse of epic poetry."

This startled me. I didn't just get music from her. When she spoke, I heard the words to songs. Others got to judge if those words were epic or not, but I was seriously beginning to think the girl was an actual Greek muse in modern form.

"West always said I was his muse. That is, until someone

else came along. And a lot of other muses came along. Most recently, Cayenne." She finished her wine with a gulp and looked around for the waitress. "But he's cheating on her already. I can tell." She rubbed her forehead and then summoned a smile for me. "So, when you called me your muse—I'm not getting involved with any more artists. I'm sorry, Bart. You're a wonderful man."

"But maybe I'm not a louse. Maybe I wouldn't cheat on you."

"You wouldn't *plan* to cheat on me. My grandfather didn't plan to cheat on my grandmother, but he did. Same with my father, who has at least two other wives and families that we know of. Once burned, twice shy, you know?"

She'd summoned the waitress and ordered another glass of wine. And in a "what the hell" gesture, she ordered a brownie sundae with extra whipped cream.

Clearly a case of transference. She wanted something she couldn't have, so she got something else. It wasn't going to satisfy her.

What she wanted was me. I was going to take care of her. I was a good guy.

An image of my mother, angry and sad and alone, floated through my brain.

I pushed it away as violently as I could. I *am* a good man, I thought. I *can* be.

Callie made it about three bites into her sundae before pushing it from her with a groan. "Eat this for me," she said, unaware of how those words could be interpreted, how badly I wanted to interpret them.

She leaned back in the booth and launched into a conversation as if we'd been discussing it all along, the way you do when you've been having impassioned, one-sided discussions in your head over and over again.

"First of all, you have to leave off the last 'untethered,'" she said, "so the song ends on, 'How could you leave me alone.' See? Just let it hang there, so the listener has to fill in the thought themselves."

She rocked me back on my heels. I'd thought I was an equal participant in the evening, and she'd suddenly ripped the floorboards out from under me. Fortunately, I was floating above the floor in my mind.

"I do see. That's an incredible idea."

"Good. Because you also need a descant on the chorus of 'Courage.' Listen."

And then, right there on the second floor of Albert's Tavern on the Saturday night before Christmas, that woman completely shifted my perception of the entire world.

She began to sing.

"'There are no wrong choices, but you have to—'"

She stopped to glare at me and I came close to violence. Her voice, a lusciously rich alto, was as warm as the fire at my back. To have heard it and then had it taken away from my life was brutal.

"Sing, Bart. You sing the melody so I can sing the harmony."

I gaped like a fish, and she reached out, put her long, slim hand on my shoulder, and nudged me.

"Do you know how much courage this is taking me? Sing. Your. Song."

I shook my head to clear it and began to sing, watching her the way a hungry lion watches an antelope.

"'There are no wrong choices, but you have to make a choice. Indecision is the killer. Sing out. I need to hear your voice. Courage.'"

Ancient muscles, unused since primitive man had fur, flexed along my spine. I was raising hackles I no longer had.

My hands were shaking. My entire nervous system turned to shining silver and pulsed with my pounding heart.

The harmony was magic. Revolutionary.

I couldn't tell where she ended and I began. It was a breathtaking combination that left me gasping.

We finished the phrase "'I need to hear your voice'"—a dangerously apt line—and silence fell. Something had shifted between us. Something had been built between us.

Then the few other upstairs patrons burst into spontaneous applause. Without realizing it, we'd begun quietly but crescendoed to power by the end.

I felt almost nauseous. It was the tickle in my belly threatening to consume me.

She looked at me, eyebrows raised. "Well?"

I tried to speak. It took a small convulsion to overcome the block in my throat. "I'm devastated." I grabbed her hand. To no longer be in physical contact with her was an impossibility. "Come with me. I have a sort of recording studio. I have to record this. Will you come with me now?"

She closed her eyes and raised her brows. Then she nodded.

15

FEATHERBED LANE

CALLIE

We were in the back of an Uber, heading into the Bronx. I still felt off-balance and otherworldly. When he'd sung his song with me, I'd felt airborne.

Like every single reason to worry or be stressed or be hyperaware was ten thousand feet beneath me, and I was soaring.

I felt him in my collarbones. That was strange, I knew. But somehow, the tugging bond I felt to him—even after we'd stopped singing—was coming from my shoulders. My core.

All right. My heart.

It's hard to be rational, to make sensible decisions when you've suddenly evolved into a new species. I think he knew I was unsure of myself because he began talking about his bike, and I absorbed every word with desperate gratitude. He was anchoring me to reality when I needed that.

"I keep the bungee cord wrapped around the frame," Bart said. "Sometimes I like the idea of riding 120 blocks in the rain. Sometimes I hate it. And riding in the snow is a whole different challenge, so I keep the bungee. That way, any Uber with a trunk can get me home."

His bike was secured behind a partially open trunk lid, the driver not minding at all.

"That's smart. If you have to bring something home that's heavy . . ."

"I can carry a lot in the panniers, but you're right. I have a model of a tree trunk I bring in every year. It would tip the bike right over." He grinned at me. "That's when it's Uber time."

"Uber time." I smiled back at him, feeling slightly drunk. On a glass and a half of wine.

And a man.

We were both slumped down on the seat, turned to face each other. The driver was on the Henry Hudson. There were long stretches when it was quite dark. Between the flashes of passing streetlights, his low voice was a caress.

"How did you do that?"

I didn't even pretend to be confused. "My father is a jazz trumpeter. There was music in my house . . . well, always."

"And you've always heard harmonies like that?"

"Never."

His hand reached out and one finger barely caressed my cheek. "Never?"

"Not until your song. I can harmonize, but just regular stuff. I've never heard anything this complex before. It kind of scared me."

"Yeah," he said softly. "It's terrifying me." His hand fell from my face. "I don't want to scare you," he said. "I have no expectations, Callie. I promise. If we can't do that again, I'll understand."

Dimly, I thought it was significant that the harmony we'd sung had taken on the importance that sex is usually accorded between two people, but it wasn't a thought I bothered to examine closely. I was too tightly aligned with his train of thought.

"I know," I told him. "I'm a little afraid we won't be able to do that again. Was it—was it as incredible as I thought? I mean, you know about music and all."

He seemed to be holding himself carefully, like a man trying not to break the eggshells under his feet. "Yeah," he breathed. "It was." He shivered. "I can still hear it, you know."

I nodded. "I can too. How is that possible?"

"When you ring a bell, it reverberates for a long time after the actual strike. The purer the bell, the longer the resonance. I think that bell had pretty spectacular resonance."

I laughed shakily. "No kidding."

He offered a bark of a laugh. "You know, sex between us will never be that good."

"How could it be?" We laughed together in perfect accord. We'd had our moment of perfect unity. If that was all we got, it would be enough.

He lived, to my amusement, on Featherbed Lane—a street not nearly as romantic or whimsical as the name would imply. The neighborhood was grim, and at this hour of the night, I was glad to have him beside me.

"I live up there," he said, nodding to a trio of windows on the second floor. "But here's why I took this place." He pulled out a set of keys and unlocked the metal shutters over the shop window in front of us. Rattling it up, he revealed an empty storefront, swept clean and bare. "Come on in." He unlocked the front door, flipped on the lights, and pulled the shutter down behind us again. "I've locked the shutter, but here's another key." A spare was hanging on a hook next to the door. "You can get out whenever you want."

"Thanks," I said, amused at his thoughtfulness but equally aware that maybe I should have been more careful about—as the mercenaries called it—securing my six.

"Most of the shops are closed along here, so no one minds this."

He stepped into the back room and flipped on the lights. A drum kit sat on a mat in the middle of the floor, surrounded by microphones and snaking cords and guitars propped on stands. Large sound baffles, the kind I'd seen in recording studios when I'd gone with my father, shaped the room into a better acoustic space.

A rough booth had been built to one side, where the sound engineer would sit.

"This has been pretty much wasted space for the last couple of years," Bart said. "Until you." He went about the room, switching on lights and instruments. "Bump and the Boys prepared for our triumphant reunion concert here. And I've been doing some writing and recording."

He meant "Untethered." And "Courage." Were there more?

Bart was in the booth, flipping switches. Then he was back, moving two microphones closer to each other.

I was standing there like a fool, watching him and not knowing what to do. He prowled toward me with sleek grace.

He slid my bag off my shoulder, and then my coat. Both were tossed on an old sofa against the wall. He took my hand and led me to one of the microphones.

"Don't think," he said as he picked up a guitar. "Whatever you do, just don't think."

I frowned at him, and he smiled in return.

"Put one hand on the microphone stand. Good. Now. Close your eyes. Go ahead."

I did it.

The sound of the guitar introduction filled my head. The space was gloriously live. He sounded like an entire orchestra. When it was time to sing the chorus, I didn't think. I sang.

So did he.

Within a few notes, I opened my eyes to see him watching me. My eyes were glistening, and the sound of the words coming out of him were wrong because he couldn't stop grinning.

"Hang on," he said, stopping us.

Then he crossed the four feet between us, slid his hand behind my back, and with his guitar between us, leaned in and kissed me.

It was different from the kisses during the blizzard. Those had been raw. Needy. This kiss went through me and made me feel like the top of my head was lifting off—but it served another purpose too. It turned the connection between us from a rope ladder to a wooden trestle. I suddenly knew we could build a stone bridge if we weren't careful.

His tongue was slow and easy on mine, and our bodies were held apart, keeping our connection in the cerebral. It was a perfect kiss.

He stepped back and shrugged philosophically. "Had to be done," he said with a grin.

"Stop talking. Play that guitar, you ass."

"Ha." He began to play.

We tried it dozens of ways. I sang my descant an octave higher, where a descant ought to be. He somehow inverted the phrases of the chorus to see what happened if the notes went up where they usually went down. He made me teach him the descant so we could see what happened when he took my part and I took his. Blissfully, we tried a take using British accents; that made us giggle so much, I was sure the recording was a waste of tape.

"Digital," he said, grinning. "Not tape. So I can manipulate it."

"Ooh, manipulation," I teased, waggling my eyebrows at him. I knew beyond a shadow of a doubt that we would end up in bed together tonight, and that the experience—despite his prediction—would not disappoint.

But I knew he was being cautious with me, giving me room to make my own decisions. Pointing out my exits, should I care to take one. He'd told me he had no expectations for the night, and that was honorable.

So, I was the one who crossed to him, slipped the guitar strap from around his neck, stood the guitar carefully in its stand, and then drew his head down to mine.

"That's enough of that part of the evening," I said before I kissed him.

"God, Callie," he said into my mouth. And then his arms were around me and he was pulling me into him.

And just like that, the rawness—the need—was back. I was almost frantic for him. No coats this time; I needed contend only with a T-shirt and jeans. Thank god.

"Sofa?" I asked.

"Fuck no," he said. "Upstairs. Back up."

As if we were in a dance company, we moved across the studio in lockstep, still buried in a greedy kiss. His hand caught the wall before I ran into it, and he moved us down to the door and into a dark hallway.

"Lights? Recording? Turn them off?" I murmured.

He took his mouth from mine long enough to say, "Fuck it and fuck it. Step up."

Oh, that changed the angle. Nice. Going up one step on the stairs, I was now a tad taller than him and leaned down to kiss him. He shifted me to the side and put his back against the wall. One long leg came up against the banister on the other side, and he was fumbling with the laces on his boot.

"You're stripping? On the stairs?"

"I'm going to do you next, so no giggling."

Of course I giggled. We both did. He was telling me nothing was less erotic than having to stop the big love scene to kick out of shoes and then wonder if your feet smelled.

He'd sat me on one of the steps above him as he said this, drawing my feet out of my sneakers and giving my instep a lingering kiss that made me shiver.

"Don't, Bart. I've had those shoes on all day."

"Mm," he hummed into my skin. "Stinky. So stinky." Then he licked me, and it was the most exciting sensation I've ever felt. "Give me the other so-stinky foot."

Helpless, I did, wishing he'd stand so I could do some licking of my own.

Then he chased me up the rest of the stairs, grabbing at my bottom. "Look at that ass move," he said. "Christ, you have a gorgeous ass, Callie."

I reached the top and stopped, my back to the door at the top. "Not as good as yours."

How did he loom over me from one step down? He fished in his pocket again for his keys. "I'm sorry. What's good?" He unlocked the door and dropped the keys inside. Then he palmed my butt and half lifted me into the hallway beyond.

I gasped, loving the sensation. "Your butt."

"My what?"

"You're an ass," I said as he kissed my neck.

"An ass with a great ass, according to you." He nibbled on a tendon. "Say it for me. Say it, Callie."

He was making me grin—and he was making me wet. "Told you you couldn't make me say it."

"Give me time." He'd reached the neckline of my shirt, but as I panted in anticipation, one strong hand slid up my back until he was tugging on my hair. He tipped my head to his and absolutely dominated me with a powerful, urgent kiss. "Welcome to my home," he murmured against my lips. "Can I get you anything?"

"Turn on the lights."

I felt him shake his head. "Too depressing."

"But I want to see you."

He literally growled. I didn't think he meant to. He reached out and flicked on a floor lamp.

We'd somehow moved from the hallway into a neat bedroom. Another guitar stood in a stand by the large bed, and a mix of photographs and paintings covered the walls. "What's depressing about this?"

"Mmph. I dunno. Just not very nice."

"I like it." I did too. Maybe because it smelled like him, fresh and clean and woodsy.

"Good," he said, losing interest in the conversation. "God, you're gorgeous, Callie."

I watched as his hands on my waist slowly slid upward. I felt like my bones were melting as he finally cupped my breasts through my shirt. It wasn't enough.

"Off," I demanded, plucking at his shirt and my buttons.

"Slow down," he murmured. "You rip all your presents open on Christmas morning all at once too?" I huffed in frustration, and he rubbed his hands rudely and divinely over my chest. "Girl, you're not big, but you sure are pretty."

Somehow, he took away all my self-consciousness about my lack of curves. His admiration was evident, and as he ground his pelvis into mine, I felt the hardness of his cock. It made my mouth water.

"Couldn't you rip open *one* present?" I asked, and he laughed at me.

"Don't you know to be careful what you ask for?" And then, with shocking speed, his two strong hands found my neckline and ripped every button off my shirt to the waist.

"Bart!" I screamed, dizzy with excitement. "How am I going to get home?"

"Wear one of my shirts. Or go like this. Make some Uber driver's day. Look at you."

My bra was plain cotton. I hadn't planned to show it off, but he was grinding against me again and that made it pretty clear he was a plain-cotton sort of guy. "Don't rip it," I gasped.

"Don't have to," he said, yanking it upward so my breasts spilled out of the bottom. Then he bent me backward over his arm and his mouth was on my nipple, his tongue flicking back and forth as he tasted.

I lost my equilibrium entirely. If he hadn't been holding me, I would have fallen.

And then I was falling. He'd pushed me back onto the bed. I lay there, dazed, as he pulled his T-shirt over his head. "Stop!" I called, and to his credit, he did stop, bare-chested next to the bed.

I scrambled off the mattress to stand in front of him, shedding the remnants of my shirt with my bra. "I've wanted this. Dreamed of it. Skin to skin, my chest to yours." I laid my breasts against him, and he groaned. He felt so good against me.

I wrapped my arms around him and drew him down to me for another kiss, getting lost in his mouth and his scent and his incredible flavor.

"My god, Callie," he murmured. "Which one of us is in charge here?"

"Both?" I said.

"Good. Okay." His hands were on my behind, cupping and caressing me, and I knew I couldn't wait to get my hands on his. It required a little maneuvering. I had to slide my arms under his to reach him, but it was worth the squirming (and the squirming was pretty enjoyable in its own right).

He exhaled heavily as I caressed his beautiful butt. "Callie," he said, his eyes closed and his head tipped back. "Where would you say you've got your pretty hands right now?"

I pinched him as hard as I could through his jeans and he laughed—until I fastened my mouth on his nipple and sucked hard. His hands closed convulsively on me, and he said in a rush, "Girl, you are begging for trouble."

"I am begging," I agreed, boldly reaching down to slide my fingers between his legs from the back.

And then I was on the bed again, my feet still on the floor. "Is this the trouble I was begging for?" I asked him saucily.

A slow grin slid over his face, and he unfastened his belt and drew it from his belt loops. I found that mildly ominous, and he saw that on my face. He held the belt suggestively, waggling his eyebrows at me, and then tossed it aside.

I was relieved . . . wasn't I?

His hand dropped to his own crotch, and he rubbed at the bulge there. "Undo your pants," he said with a certain throaty menace.

I was going to say no—I had every intention—until I realized my traitor hands had drifted to my waist.

"Good girl," he rumbled. "Go on. Show me."

"You're very demanding, aren't you?"

"Yeah. Go on."

I unsnapped my jeans and slid the zipper down, my mouth dry and my heart pounding.

"Look at you. Bare breasted on my bed. Tug 'em down a little. That's good. Now raise up that pretty ass."

He'd gotten me out of my jeans without a single awkward moment, but now I was lying naked in front of him, and he still had his pants on. "Now you?" I asked.

"In a minute."

He fell to his knees and ran his hands all over my torso. "Your skin is so soft. You've almost got a nap to you—like velvet. Feel it? I pet you like this"—his hand swept from the point of one hip to the other—"and it feels like I'm standing up the velvet." He moved his hand to my belly button and began a slow slide down to my pubic bone. "And like this, you're silk. So incredibly smooth."

He leaned down, his shaggy hair tickling me, and pressed kisses to my skin where his hand had been.

"I'm like iron in my jeans right now," he said casually as he kissed my belly, his fingers sliding down to find the slippery cleft at the center of me. "You'd better not touch me yet. I'd go off like a fucking rocket. My lord, you smell like heaven."

His mouth had followed his fingers. Without any teasing and with no hurry, he was somehow both fingering and licking me. I found my feet on his shoulders, fully open to him.

"And your flavor . . ." He licked long, from my clit to the entrance. "You're incredible. Why are you so delicious?"

He didn't seem to need an answer, which was lucky, as I was incapable of thought, much less speech.

"Pretty soon, I'm going to show you what you've done to me, lying here all wet and ready. My cock is going to burst, but I'm going to make sure it bursts right in here."

His fingers opened me easily as his tongue flicked relentlessly against my clitoris. As if from a million miles away, I marveled at what he was doing to me. I'd never been ready so quickly for West. Now I could feel an orgasm building in me with undeniable force; it almost scared me.

"Bart," I gasped.

"What?" he said, lifting his face from me and replacing his tongue with one large, callused finger. "You got something to say, counselor?"

"Oh, god—"

"Mm. Like hearing that. What do you say to this?"

His fingers thrust into me faster, and his thumb ground the tiny, brilliant nerve endings of my clit into the bone behind them. I cried out.

"What?" he asked cruelly. "What did you say?"

"Bart—more!"

"More? Like this?"

"Oh my god!" And then I was incapable of speech as my orgasm bloomed within me, the sudden shocking heat of a wildfire racing past any control.

As all my nerve endings reordered themselves into their proper places, he was kissing the inside of my thigh, working his way slowly down to my knee. "Callie," he breathed. "Callie, you're doing things to me."

"You're the one doing things to me," I panted. "Give me a minute and that will change."

He looked up at me with a grin. "What? What does that mean?"

"I'm going to want to see your cock. Then I'm going to want to inspect it. Very closely. With my tongue."

His head jerked back as he took in those words. "God, I almost came, just hearing you say *cock*. You're a naughty thing, aren't you?"

"Come here and find out."

He shook his head. "I wasn't kidding. I'm far too close. You want to use your mouth on me any other time, I'm definitely the guy for you. But not tonight. Not now. It's Christmas, baby, and I want all my presents."

He stood and put his hands to the button of his jeans—then, thinking twice, he turned and regarded me with a grin over his shoulder. He slowly and deliberately wiggled his butt at me.

I laughed even as I got breathless. "Go ahead," I said. "I'd like a striptease."

He dropped his jeans down his hips with agonizing slowness, revealing a taut, muscled ass. All that bike riding, I thought, was really paying off.

"Gluteus minimus," I said as the waistband dipped, "looking good. And here's glute medius. Oh, that's nice. And voilà—gluteus maximus, in absolutely spectacular form. Bart, your posterior is magnificent."

He tugged the jeans back up again and turned to me in exasperation.

I laughed at him. "Thank you," I said. "That was even lovelier than I expected."

He regarded me in mock disappointment. Then he

threw himself down on his side next to me. "Even lovelier," he repeated. "You are a stubborn woman."

He leaned down to lick at my breasts and I arched into his mouth, feeling my nerve endings come alive again. Then he hissed in his breath when I slid my hand to his waist . . . beneath the open waistband . . . and finally, at last, after too long, my fingers met the velvet-over-steel head of his cock.

"There you are," I breathed.

"Have mercy," he said. "I don't want to shoot off like a kid. Don't tease me, Callie, please."

"I just want to feel," I couldn't help but purr as I felt the length of him. He was larger than West had been, even at his best, and felt incredible in my hand. I wrapped my fingers as best I could around him and tugged gently to pull the loose skin upward.

He jerked against me and pulled back and out of my hand. "Callie," he said as if my name was a curse. And then his hand came down on my crotch again, slipping and sliding through the wet flesh until he'd taken full possession of me. "Callie, I've got to fuck you. Fuck you or die. Are you ready?"

"I'm ready. I'm so ready."

He let go of me, and it was agonizing to lose his heat and pressure. He reached into the drawer of his bedside table and found a condom. We hadn't had the awkward talk, and now I was glad we didn't have to.

He fumbled and cursed, and I pinched his side hard. He reared back and glared at me.

"Stopped you from coming, didn't it?" I grinned.

"You minx. You're going to get it." He rolled on top of me, pinning me to the bed. I struggled for the fun of realizing that he was so strong.

"Get it? Get that trouble you were talking about?" I was

definitely breathless as I spoke, feeling a desperate, yawning emptiness inside me.

He'd nudged my legs apart and was lying on top of me, the head of his cock close to my center. My breath shortened. I was panting.

"Trouble. Right," he grunted. He tugged my hands upward so he could hold both wrists with one hand. With the other, he reached between us and seated his cock against me.

"Do you want this, Callie?"

"Yes," I breathed.

"Callie, open your eyes. Look at me."

I did. He held my gaze.

"Do you want me to fuck you?"

"Yes. Yes, Bart."

"Say it, then."

"Bart! Not now!"

He shook his head, implacable. "You say it or you don't get it."

"Do it," I begged. "I'm getting desperate."

He refused to move. I tried to thrust my hips upward to impale myself on him, but he wouldn't let me. "Say it."

"You're making me angry, Bart. Do it. Put it in me."

"Well, that's good, but it's not what I want to hear." He was panting, both from his own excitement and from having to hold me down as I writhed. "Say it, Callie."

"Goddamn it, Bart!"

"Say it. Say it, Callie, or I won't do it."

"Bart, you bastard! *Fuck* me, all right? Fuck me right now!"

His cock slammed into me, and I began coming almost immediately. I screamed. It was like being electrocuted—I jittered helplessly around him as he plunged into me.

I think he made it into me three times—three pounding strokes before he, too, was shouting wordlessly. And then we were both lost, the connection between us like golden ropes of fire burning along every nerve. It went on and on. I think I had a second orgasm almost before the first one stopped.

I reached up and bit him on his shoulder—not a loving nip but a full bite I couldn't release until, to my horror, I tasted blood.

I think I died for a moment after that. At least, I lost consciousness. When awareness returned, I was floating on euphoria.

Bart tried to roll off me, and I found I had some muscle control after all. I grabbed him, wrapping my arms and legs around him. "Don't move," I panted. "Give me a minute. I'll fly apart if you're not on top of me."

"I'll crush you," he said.

"Good. I need to be crushed a little."

I held him, relishing the heat and strength and weight of him until he broke through my limpet grip by reminding me he needed to retrieve the rubber.

Right. Go ahead.

"You bit the shit out of me," he said admiringly as he returned to the bed.

"I'm sorry about that," I said. "I didn't mean to."

"Never bitten anyone in the throes before?" He pulled the blankets down from underneath me and rolled me under the covers.

"Never," I said, feeling wonderfully lazy. He gathered me to him, my head on his chest and his knee between mine.

"Good," he said. "It was exciting, but I'd rather not be covered with your bite marks when I go back to school."

"Mm," I sighed. "I could bite you where no one would

see." It made me grin that he jerked involuntarily at the thought.

We were dozing and perhaps heading for real sleep when I nudged him.

"Ha," he responded indistinctly.

"Bart—Bart." He opened one eye and regarded me. "I've only ever had sex with West before. This didn't feel like that."

"Better or worse?"

"As God is my witness, Your Honor, better. So much better. Was it just that West wasn't very good? Or was this—you know—special?"

He rolled so he and I were facing each other. "Did you ever harmonize with anyone the way you harmonize with me?"

I shook my head gravely.

"Baby, this was special. This was explosive. We're never going to be able to duplicate this."

But we did. Twice more that night, and once again before I dressed in one of his T-shirts and took him back to my apartment. And then things got complicated.

16

TRUTHS

CALLIE

One of his guitars took up a position in my apartment. A bottle of my shampoo appeared in his shower. I told my best friends about him, and Rita insisted on a group call with Bart. They gave him the third degree and insisted I have him call Mimi so she could weigh in too. After that exhaustive interrogation, Cleo and Rita declared themselves satisfied. “He can stay,” they said.

Bart and I were inseparable, spending almost every moment together when I wasn’t at work.

When we weren’t rutting like animals, he would work on his music while I prepped for the AresCorp case. His presence soothed me. I could focus more sharply and accomplish more work with him in the next room.

Even my team noticed I was handling the stress with greater ease. “What’s up with you?” Carla asked. “That’s a brilliant piece of analysis, even for you. Are you on one of those brain enhancers?”

I smiled. “I guess I’m focusing more while Leigh is with her father.”

"How's she doing?" Carla knew about Leigh and a bit about my ex-husband. With a shock, I realized that Carla, and to a lesser extent Jesse, had become almost friends.

"She's doing pretty well. She's happy to see her old friends, and her father is on his best behavior."

"That's great. Good for her. And good for you! You have got it going on with this judicial request."

My relationship with my team was improving daily, and they began to feel comfortable coming to me with ideas of their own. Areas of specialty suggested themselves, and—it was hard for me to countenance it, but it was true—a fragile trust formed between us.

The downside was that all our powerful success was attracting Lawrence's attention too. Either that or I was putting out a subliminal well-fucked vibe, and he was picking up on it.

(I was definitely going to slip up and curse in front of a jury. Bart was so turned on when I used profane language that I was getting entirely too comfortable with phrases like *well-fucked*.)

(I was also getting used to being well fucked.)

Lawrence summoned me to his office one evening after the New Year. "Ms. Lyndon," he said, waving me to my accustomed seat as I came in. "I wanted to congratulate you. This motion for dismissal is extremely well researched."

"It won't work," I said.

"No, but it will lay the groundwork for our defense."

"That's what I thought too."

"We're beginning to move in sync," he said, his voice dropping to an intimate tone. "It's exciting, don't you think?"

"Great legal minds," I said in the hopes that I could keep this on a professional level.

"Great minds," he corrected me. "Compatibility. You can't find that just anywhere."

He wasn't touching me—he wasn't anywhere near me—but I could hear it in his voice, see it in the way he leaned toward me. This was what we might refer to as an inappropriate conversation in cases of human resources.

It was the first time in my life I'd ever been grateful to hear Addie Belle's high heels clicking down the hallway. She appeared in Lawrence's suite, breezing past his executive secretary with a wave of her fluttering fingers.

"Sweetness, are y'all ready for our dinner? Oh—Callie. How nice to see you, darlin."

Her husband and I had a desk between us; she couldn't read anything into our meeting. I nodded to her. "Shall we table this for tomorrow?" I asked him.

"Fine," he replied, his tone not changing but his meaning doing a complete reversal. "Again, this is a nice motion, Callie. Well done. Have a good night."

Dismissed, I left, refusing to skitter past Addie Belle as if she were venomous. "Good night, Addie Belle."

"Ciao ciao," she said with her sweetest smile. I gave her a tiny nod. I heard her very clearly. Addie Belle and her phone photos.

It was with great relief that I remembered I was scheduled for a late dinner with Bump, Pandora, and Bart. On the agenda: discussing ways to break it to Leigh that her mother and the bio teacher she had a crush on were wrapped around each other like snakes on a medical caduceus. It was worrying me, and she was due back in two days.

So, even though it was only eight, I dismissed my team with my compliments, advising them to enjoy an early night. They cheered. We rode down in the elevator together. It was so collegial that I had two minutes of regret when I got out at the lobby for the car service and they continued to the basement for the subway.

But taking the car service to the Bronx was a far more enjoyable mode of transportation than the rattling, overheated subway—even if you often could get from here to there faster underground than you ever could on the surface.

Unless you had a bike, of course.

I had no reason to feel smug. The chances of me biking anywhere were minimal at best, but I felt a burst of possessive pride at the thought of my lover biking with an environmentalist's pure heart and a Greek god's ass to save the planet.

Bump rented, somewhat improbably, an old Gulfstream trailer hooked up to services in an empty lot under the Cross Bronx Expressway. It was surprisingly cozy. He said it reminded him of many of the places he'd lived in Vermont, and he wished he could persuade Panda and Fonse to move in with him.

"Too small," Panda said, avoiding him as he reached for her hip. She put a platter of empanadas on the table. Bart and I were comfortably ensconced on the bench seat. It was like being in a slightly worn yacht. "You get a bigger place, we'll talk."

"Money talks," he sighed. "I can't do much more on the deli salary."

"How about picking up a few gigs?" Bart asked casually.

Bump rounded on him. "You want to gig? We're not too old?"

"Speak for yourself, old man." They teased each other for a while, and then Bart said, ever so casually, "I'm up to six new songs we could work on."

There was silence in the trailer, and then Panda let out

an excited yip. Bump leaned over and extended his hand . . . to me. "You are *so good* for him," he said with a grin.

"She is," Bart confirmed, pulling me closer. "But I wrote the songs, so fuck you."

"Yeah. Fuck me. That's a damned good empanada, babe."

"Of course it is. I want to teach Leigh and her friends how to make them," she said to me. "You think they could come up here after school?"

The neighborhood, while grim, would be safe for them during the day, as long as they stayed in the deli. Bart worked out the logistics.

"I can Uber home with them after school, and then you can pick them up when you're ready."

"That sounds great," I said. It might help Leigh, I thought, to not hate me as much when she found out about Bart. "But I'm going to be working some pretty late hours. I've got an enemy to foil, after all."

Surprised, they clamored for details and were dumbstruck when I told them the boss's wife thought I wanted to apply to be Boss's Wife Number Three—or was it Number Four?

"Your boss is Lawrence McCrillis," Bart said, astonished. "So you're talking about Addie Belle?"

"One and the same. Do you know," I explained to Bump and Panda, "that she's got all her friends spying for her? Half the committee heads for the talent show are reporting directly back to her. I'm keeping secrets from *everyone* to stop her from sabotaging me."

"Jesus," Panda said. "You need another empanada. We need to get this bitch."

"Or we could kill off the husband," Bart offered. "I'm not too pleased with him in this."

"No, don't kill Lawrence. I need him. I've got to win this case."

"To make partner. I remember the bet. You win the case and make more than $1.06 million at the talent show, and he gets you an office with a window."

I thought with a pang that I hadn't shared with him the update—that I was now fighting for a good recommendation from Lawrence at some other law office. Anywhere, as long as it wasn't New York City. Either that or Addie Belle would get me fired.

How this would affect my relationship with Bart was an open question. I wanted to continue with him; there was no doubt. But could I keep the man and lose the city?

I was still trying to work it out later that night as Bart and I were tangled up in bed, breathing each other's air. He'd just defined a new outer limit to how hard I could orgasm (again), and I had a very clear understanding in every muscle of how a wet washcloth felt. Once I'd regained the ability to think, I bit lightly at his chest until he grunted, and then I said, "I like being with you."

As attuned to me as he was, he realized this wasn't an idle statement. "Same goes. Except maybe for the biting thing."

I thought about it. "Are we edging closer to a declaration?"

I felt his heartbeat pick up a bit.

"Waiting on you, Callie. Not going to scare you off."

That made my pulse go faster too. I nestled impossibly closer. "Thank you, Bart."

"I'd fight dragons for you, girl."

"I'd fight 'em for you too."

"Declaration enough for now. Go to sleep."

With school starting in two days, he had work to do, so I had the car service drop him off at Hamilton on my way to work the next day. His soft kiss through the window curled my toes and started my day right.

The glow lasted until before lunch, when I heard those high heels clacking toward me. I rolled my eyes and asked my team to give me a few minutes. They filed out of my office as Addie Belle walked up.

"My goodness, look at all of you! Aren't you an impressive bunch! And with such a clever leader! It's pretty Callie, youngest associate to take on such a major case!" She shut the door behind her and dropped her winsome ways. "I don't want you to think for one minute that I don't know what you're doing. Lawrence is incapable of more than half a woody without pharmaceutical assistance, the old fart, and he was hard yesterday after you left. You can be sure I checked."

I winced. Conversations with Addie Belle never worked out well for me. This one was particularly revolting.

"You're going to pay for this attempt to steal him."

"Addie Belle, I'm not—"

"Not another word. You try it again, and I'll have your daughter branded a disciplinary case. She won't be able to get into a decent school anywhere in the free world." She launched an arrogant eyebrow at me, and I felt my ire overwhelm my common sense.

"You'll leave my daughter out of this."

She sniffed her contempt. "You still think we're playing by Good Girl rules. That's why you're going to lose. The talent show is in two months. The case should come to court about the same time. That's your deadline, darlin'. Don't miss it."

She turned, but as she put her hand on the doorknob, she paused. Over her shoulder, she tossed her last poison dart.

"We had an early board meeting at the school this morning. I saw you drop off Barton Thetford. Very touching. Have you fucked him yet?" She turned, and her cruel smile was a warning to steel for something horrible. "Try talking dirty to him while he's fucking you. I always did. It spurs him to greater heights, if you know what I mean."

She was gone, and I was ruined.

17

NUMBNESS IS EASY

BART

I was surprised and delighted to find Callie in her apartment. It was only a little after five, and I'd used the key she'd given me. I'd planned to wait for her to get home while I got in a few hours on a jazz-fusion thing inspired by the strip of skin behind her ear. I wasn't sure how commercial the song would be, but I couldn't ignore it. It was demanding to come out of my guitar.

This was our last evening together before Leigh came home. I assumed Callie had come home early so we could sing or laugh or fuck or tease. Hopefully, all four.

And then I saw her and knew none of those things would happen that night.

She hadn't turned on any of the lights. It was clear she'd been sitting there since before the dull January afternoon had turned into an early evening. A box and my guitar in its case were beside her on the sofa. I felt a bolt of pure panic.

"Callie?"

She turned to me, absolutely calm on the surface and her eyes all but dead. "Are you fucking Addie Belle?"

The world collapsed under my feet. Like a truck going over a bridge, everything slowed down to a crawl. All my possible answers flashed through my mind, and all were rejected. For Callie—for myself—nothing but raw, bitter truth would do.

"Not anymore."

She closed her eyes. It was her only reaction. She'd been braced for my response.

I stood in her living room feeling as if my arms were too long. My molars hurt. Nothing felt right. I waited for her judgment, a feeling of doom swamping me. I'd seen Addie Belle at the school that morning but avoided her. Or so I thought.

"When was the last time?"

Miserable, I answered. "After the field trip. That afternoon."

Her eyes opened, her accusation blazing in her deep brown eyes. "You fucked Addie Belle after writing 'Courage' in my car? After we went through that with you?"

I felt a prickle of anger. "After you fled when I called you a muse, yes. I went into the school once the kids were gone and she was there, and I was jacked up from the song and from you and upset that you'd run away, and there she was."

"So you fucked her."

I shrugged, deflated. "She fucked me, if you must know."

"Was that the only time?"

Could it possibly get worse? "No."

There was absolutely no humor in her laugh. "Why? Why Addie Belle?"

My knees gave out, and I sat in a straight chair against the wall. "I don't know. She was married. There wouldn't be any complications. She didn't need anything but a fuck. She was cute and easy and there. I wasn't hurting anyone. I just did it."

"Addie Belle is *cute*?" Callie betrayed more pain with that question than she'd shown me since she came in.

"Callie, she's nothing. She never was."

"She's absolutely everything that I am not. And you are everything I feared. This is all your stuff. Take it. We'll never mention anything to Leigh. We're done. Do you have any questions?"

She raised her dispassionate corporate-shark face to me, and I knew I'd lost her.

The world went silent.

I saw her often after that. We met over the talent show. I ran rehearsals, and we had to decide the order of performances. She behaved with perfect decorum. She was polite and outwardly friendly, helpful, and inspiring. Everyone we worked with was impressed with her, and the kids actively began to seek her out.

But there was a wall of ice around her that could not be breached. I didn't even try.

Bump was the only one who cried. I confessed my sins to him and Panda one evening before the deli closed. Fonse was asleep on his cot in the storeroom. "I fucked up. Again. I lost her. And I can't hear the music anymore," I said in summation.

And Bump started to cry.

“Come on, man,” I said. “We were doing fine before I wrote those songs. We’ll be fine now.”

Bump walked out. No coat, no umbrella, nothing. Just Bump and a sleety night.

“He’s not crying about the music, you fuckwit,” Panda said with pitying contempt. “He’s crying for you. You’re such a shit.”

She stomped back to the kitchen, and I sat there alone in the deli, willing to agree but having no one to say it to.

Callie and Panda arranged the cooking lessons. Either Leigh, Shane, and Olivia Ubered to the Bronx with me or Callie paid for a car service to take them, and the car service brought them home again. Twice, when she had the day off, Panda took Fonse to Callie’s apartment so they could cook there.

Of course, I knew when it was happening, but I made sure to be far away during the actual lessons. Being in a place of warmth and light and good smells felt alien to me. Better to sit in my apartment, where I could manage the atmosphere and ignore the empty studio downstairs.

I’d come to hate late January. It was a great time when I was growing up; there was skiing and snowshoes and my friends and I would work on an eternal snow-fort kingdom in one of our pastures that grew throughout the winter into a tiny, boy-ruled metropolis.

But in New York City, late January meant dirty tatters of

snow and sleeting, icy rain and darkness that fell almost before school got out.

And it meant my mother's birthday.

Life is easier once you're numb. Friday after school, I took the subway out to the lot in New Jersey where I paid to keep my old beater of a pickup. I had to get the kid at the gate to give me a jump, but it started up eventually, and I headed north.

No breakdowns. No speeding tickets (because I sure wasn't speeding). Traffic wasn't too bad going around Albany. Night fell quickly, but that suited my mood anyway. I turned on the radio, but the music felt harsh to my ears, and I switched to talk radio, which I could ignore.

One of the crappy motels on the fringe of Burlington had a room. I slept there.

The next morning, I stopped at the grocery store for flowers. She liked licorice. I got her a box.

I drove up to the retirement community. "Samantha Thetford," I told the man at the front gate. He buzzed me in.

There was a quilting circle in the lobby, and a few residents were piecing together jigsaw puzzles by the big fireplace. It was cheery and warm.

But Mom was sitting alone in the living room of her apartment, looking out the window.

"I saw you drive up. Still have your truck, huh?"

I kissed her papery cheek and handed her the flowers.

"Put them in some water, will you, Barton? There's a vase in the kitchen cabinet."

I wasn't good at polite conversation, and she had nothing to say to me. We sat in silence for an eternity, two large, empty places sitting with us. The tick of her grandmother's cuckoo clock was the only sound, counting out the seconds to her death. I had no idea where I got the courage to speak.

"Mom, are you ever going to forgive me?"

She looked around at me, and I saw, to my surprise, that her eyes were full of tears.

"I wish you'd died instead of your sister."

Hearing it was no worse than thinking it. It was a relief to have her say it out loud, while she looked into my eyes at last. In return, I gave her the raw, bitter truth.

"I wish I had too."

There was second of utter stillness between us—and then, like I'd been assassinated, I was rocked back in my chair by the assault of horrific, pained, shrieking music that filled my head. My creative block was gone.

18

IGNORING DESPAIR

CALLIE

I was far too busy to be sad. I had no time for anything like that.

I went to Washington to pick up my daughter. Leigh's return filled me with frantic happiness; I couldn't get enough of her. She'd missed me, too, and we spent the entire train ride home and the rest of the evening trying to bridge a two-week gap.

She told me about her friends from her old school, and how our old apartment building had gotten new furniture in the lobby, and—hesitantly—about her father and Susan.

"She misses you, I'm sure of it," Leigh said.

I sighed. "I miss her. But she made her choice. Do you really call her Cayenne?"

Leigh sniggered. "Did you know she wanted to call herself Cheyenne, like the capital of Wyoming, but got the spelling wrong?"

This struck me as hysterical. It was as if that one stupid mistake summed up, in a few missed letters, the entire end of both my marriage and my friendship. I didn't know why that should make me feel better, but I felt an old weight become smaller. Like the dissolution of my former life was becoming trivial to me. A misspelling.

We talked about the talent show and the news that the two families from Syria were scheduled to arrive in Sweden in February.

"You're going over there?"

"Taking half my team. It will only be for a few days, and Mrs. Kim will stay with you."

"Can't I go too?"

"To Sweden in February? Believe me, you don't want to go. Besides, you have to run the talent show while I'm gone."

"Mr. Thetford can do that."

I was proud that I didn't even twitch. "He'll need your help."

"All right. But bring me something."

"What?"

"I don't know. I'll have to research what they have." She made me smile. I was so proud of her.

To my surprise, I was also proud of my team at Hoare Ascutney. They'd shaped up to be an effective force, and I only rarely daydreamed about executing them all once I made partner.

Carla and Jesse had become trusted lieutenants over the months we'd worked together, and they were pretty sharp-eyed. I hadn't realized they'd read my stress until one afternoon not long before we left for Sweden, when they asked for a closed-door meeting.

We sat in my little office, and I regarded them with curiosity.

"What if," Jesse said, "you knew of someone who'd had their juvenile records expunged when they turned eighteen?"

Jesse had the makings of a good corporate lawyer. He always spoke as if he were on the record—a smart way for a lawyer to live their life.

"I would wonder why that mattered to me."

Carla nodded. "What if it were me Jesse was talking about?"

The problem with entirely hypothetical conversations is that you can wander in circles before stumbling onto the right avenue of investigation.

"If that were the case, what questions do you feel would be appropriate for me to ask?"

Jesse took that one. "Perhaps you could ask what sorts of crimes were expunged from the juvenile record."

I nodded thoughtfully. "All right. In this entirely hypothetical case, tell me about the nature of the crimes."

Carla took a deep breath and clearly made a leap of trust. "What if I was a hacker in high school? I mean, like, good enough to have attracted federal attention?"

Carla wasn't quite as good as Jesse at the hypothetical, but the conversation was certainly holding my interest.

"That would be surprising, given the exacting security clearances all junior associates must pass in order to be offered employment at Hoare Ascutney."

"Certainly," Carla agreed while Jesse nodded. "Unless the hacker had gotten smarter, and certain information was repressed. Not to deceive," she hastened to add, "but to give, um, the employee applicant the opportunity to reform and start fresh."

"Admirable. Illegal but admirable."

"There are times, you'll stipulate," Jesse said, "when bending the law can produce enough value to be worth the risk." I noticed for the first time that he was holding a plain manila folder.

They had information, illegally obtained, and wanted to know if I wanted in on the secrets in that folder. Given the nature of our case, this could turn dangerous quickly; we were dancing around the State Department at the least. I needed to tread carefully.

"I will stipulate that. In a purely hypothetical way, which parties do you assume would be most damaged by that value, and which would be most greatly benefited?"

Carla and Jesse exchanged looks, and she nodded at him. Then he floored me.

"Addie Belle McCrillis to the former and you to the latter," he said flatly. "Hypothetically."

Holy Jesus, mother of God. Great googly-moogly. What the frick. No, this was definitely time for profanity. What the fuck.

I had a good poker face. All successful corporate lawyers have to. My inner turmoil was expressed in a raised eyebrow. "Interesting."

Carla took the folder from Jesse. "Yes, it is," she said. "Very interesting."

She made a movement as if to offer me the file, and I shook my head. "No, thank you. Not at this time. I would like time to reflect, if you don't mind."

"Of course. Accessory after the fact of the commission of a crime is worth sober reflection," Jesse said. He grabbed Carla's elbow and they stood to leave, taking their manila temptation with them. At the door, he turned. "We're on your side, Callie. Just so you know."

Fortunately, he closed the door behind them before I began to cry.

The question of my legal ethics was forced to take a lower priority, and I was glad of it. With a cheating father and a cheating ex-husband, I believed I was fundamentally committed to truth. I'd been drawn to the law for its emphasis on justice. It was startling to realize that one manila folder could tempt me away from an aspect of my personality that I had considered inviolate.

The trip to Sweden to depose the two witnesses in the AresCorp case was a welcome distraction. To avoid any improprieties, we traveled with and stayed within conversational range of the Human Rights Watch lawyer and her assistant, and we were accompanied by an assistant deputy from the State Department to handle any diplomatic considerations.

The journey was surprisingly exhausting and exceedingly depressing. The sun never rises in that part of Sweden in the winter. The Syrians looked shell-shocked by that and by the cold, but the wife of one of the witnesses held my hand and told me, through an interpreter, how deeply grateful she was to have gotten her family out. We both cried as she spoke. The Human Rights Watch lawyer raised an eyebrow but made no comment.

The depositions were grim. I was even surer in my personal conviction that the two AresCorp employees had gone on a shooting spree, gunning down innocent civilians in a gun-fueled rage, but that line of thinking was not how I would best serve my client, AresCorp. I kept Lawrence apprised by email and Zoom, and he made sure I stayed grounded in what was important.

We were waiting at the airport for our flight home when the Human Rights Watch lawyer approached me. "Callie," she said, "I just got the news." She read an email from her phone. "You remember the third witness? The nurse who wouldn't leave Syria?"

Dread in my heart, I nodded.

"She was killed last night. Her hospital was bombed by the government. We can strike her from the list of witnesses."

I was cold. Exhausted. Appalled. Horrified. I felt quite shockingly alone. But I had a great poker face. "Thank you for informing me. I'll tell my team."

She nodded and went back to her seat.

The plane wasn't even half full. Once the flight took off, we all scattered to have room for sleep (or, in my case, work). I sat in a middle row of four seats with emptiness all around me and began by checking my email. Amid the dozens of work-related messages and updates from the talent show committee chairs, I flagged two of personal interest—one from Leigh and one from West.

I needed a boost. I started with Leigh.

To: Mom

From: Leigh

Subject: Email sucks

I don't see why I can't text you when you're in Sweden. It's all the same satellite.

A bunch of people are going to the movies on Friday night. Shane and Olivia are going. Can I go?

P.S. Trevor Woodley asked me to go. I think this is my first date. It's a group date, which is appropriate for a girl my age. I looked it up. You don't have to worry. He is REALLY CUTE.

. . .

I felt a pang for my girl going on her first date—and I was excited for her. Growing up was inevitable. I certainly wanted to be involved in her decisions, and I was glad I'd be around on Friday to return the favor on the Style Council and consult with her on which sweater, shoes, and the like.

And I suppressed any thought that her crush on her bio teacher—no need to label him with a first name—seemed to be over.

She'd made me smile. I felt ready for West's message.

To: Calla

From: Westmore

Subject: Wonderful News!

Sorceress Calla lily, my sculpture of my darling mini muse has been purchased by the Whitney Museum in your adopted city and will be installed in their sculpture garden in March. Our beautiful Leigh's face will forever brighten the Big Apple. It's the right setting for the jewel you and I made together.

My love, I want to see you. I miss you like a torch out of acetylene. I am tragic, limp, useless without you beside me. I am done with anyone less magnificent than you—anyone less inspirational. Come with me to the opening next month. Be my muse once more.

I hope it does not need to be said that the former Cayenne (now plain Susan once more) has departed from my life and my interest. You and our little girl are the only muses in my heart. Tell me I can come see you. Say the word and I'm on a plane tonight.

I cannot endure if I am not with you again. All my love – West

West wanted me back. I was left mute and paralyzed, compelled to read his words over and over again. They'd come at a time when I most urgently needed them—when I felt unloved and unlovable, when my career and relationships had left me unbalanced and uneasy, when the future looked bleak and alone as my daughter blossomed and grew away from me.

My finger hovered over the Reply button. How I longed for West to sweep in and make everything better. How I longed, a deep yearning in me like the moon's pull on the tides, to surrender to the easiest path. To lay down my burdens and fears and let him think for me.

I was so tired of figuring everything out.

The one thing that stopped me was the thought of that Syrian nurse, who'd stubbornly gotten herself killed because she wouldn't stop caring for her community.

She didn't take the easy path. She took the hard path, not because it was safe. Far from it; it was profoundly dangerous. She did it because it was right.

She died for her strength, and if I didn't carry on her strength, it would be like a portion of her determination rippling through the world would be weakened and lost.

So, I took a deep breath on that dark airplane and decided on a new plan.

Maybe Superwoman would be better if she had a team, after all.

Jesse and Carla were dozing with an empty seat between them. I woke them up when I fought past Carla to plop down. They woke up, startled.

"All right. What do you have? Give it to me."

Jesse took one look at my face and convulsed forward to pull his cloth computer case from under the seat in front of him. He slid the manila folder out and handed it to me as Carla silently clapped her hands in excitement. They both leaned over when I snapped on the overhead light to read what they'd found.

It was the prenuptial agreement between Lawrence and Addie Belle.

I gasped and looked to Carla. She waggled her eyebrows at me. "It wasn't even hard. Internet security at Hoare Ascutney is shit. Look at this part."

They walked me through an agreement that was all about business and nothing about love. Addie Belle would be paid three million for giving birth to a boy, one million for a girl; Carla and I exchanged looks of fury over this monetizing of sexism. Jesse tapped the paper urgently, drawing my attention down to a later passage.

"Look. Pay attention. See here? If they divorce, she gets one million dollars for every year she stayed married to him. If she makes it to ten years, the amount automatically doubles to a cap of twenty million. Look at when it's dated. Eight and a half years ago."

He watched me as I worked it out. Carla spoke the obvious. "If she lasts with him another eighteen months—well, sixteen now—she gets an additional twelve million. I'd call that a motive for threatening you."

"How did you know she was threatening me?"

Carla rolled her eyes. "I sit right outside your office. Everyone thinks no one can hear you if you shut the door. There's an air vent right by the fucking door. Sheesh."

I was dumbfounded, but there was one more nugget of unpolished gold for them to point out.

Carla did the honors. "Right here," she said, pointing with a bitten nail.

"Parties agree that . . . until such time as . . . wherefore the agreement will be . . . hereafter . . . holy shit."

"She got to it." Jesse smiled.

"She did," Carla agreed.

I looked up. "If she has an affair, she loses everything."

"Everything." They spoke together, an echo at either ear.

Carla went on, "Even the three million for birthin' a precious man-baby. I think I overheard her talking about—um, an affair she's been having."

My mind had gone into vapor lock. "You didn't record her conversation with me, did you?"

"Nope. But if I understood things, she's not the only one who could testify to her infidelity. Is she?"

Bart.

Bart could be the reason Addie Belle's prenup would be declared null and void.

"Oh my fucking god," I said quietly.

"You're damned right," Jesse said.

"What are you going to do?" Carla asked.

My mind was whirling. I needed time. "I don't know yet. But I'll keep you posted. Thank you." I leaned over and kissed Carla's cheek and then did the same to Jesse. "You're both amazing."

I stood, and Carla moved her legs to help me escape the seat. "Now," I said, "I need some legal advice from someone I respect."

The Human Rights Watch lawyer was sleeping a few rows back. She was about to be woken up.

Two emails got to the US long before I did. Both of them lightened the shadow on my heart, and I delighted in imagining the responses to both of them.

. . .

To: Leigh

From: Mom

Subject: Re: Email sucks

I'm excited about your first date! Of course you can go. Thank you for telling me. You'll indulge me, I'm sure, while I tell you what I want you to know about how you deserve to be treated by boys. I'm ordering my thoughts on that score. I'll be ready to discuss with you before your date.

Also, save me some time this evening. I have a story I want to tell you. Home soon. All my love – Mom.

To: Westmore

From: Callie

Subject: Re: Wonderful News!

West, congratulations on the sale of Leigh's sculpture. All of New York will rightly revere it.

I'm attaching an itemized list of your back child-support payments, as well as an accounting of the $174,000 in credit card debt the judge assigned to me in our divorce. I've paid down $34,000. I expect you to pay the rest; you spent it, after all. Now that the Whitney has bought Leigh's sculpture, I'm sure you'll be able to afford payment. As your price for all remaining work will rise accordingly, I know you'll be able to maintain an elevated payment schedule in the future.

I warned Susan what she was getting into with you. Some lessons can't be learned without personal experience.

I'd be delighted to come to the opening. Leigh will be my date. See you then. Callie

Leigh wasn't surprised when I told her about my brief relationship with Bart once I got home.

"I'm not an idiot, Mom. I knew about it."

"You did? How?"

"Because I know you. You were super happy for a while, and then you were miserable. He turned into an ice cube and never smiled. It was pretty obvious. You were acting the way girls do when they break up with someone they care about, and who else was it going to be? He's super good-looking."

"You're so smart."

"I know."

"And you're not upset?"

"Why? Because I liked him? Nah. He was too old for me."

"Not like Trevor Woodley, huh?"

"Wait, want to see Trevor? Look—Shane took this photo at lunch. Oh my God, look at this. This is him—not this guy. That's his twin. I think Trevor is cuter, don't you?"

I let her excitement wash away my anxiety. I had a lot to accomplish, but for the first time in a while, I felt proud of the direction I was heading in.

19

THE TALENT SHOW

CALLIE

Leigh made me go shopping and talked me into a beautiful cream-silk dress for the talent show. It wasn't my style at all, with a halter top and a swishy skirt, but I felt different when I wore it. More feminine and powerful at the same time. Knowing I'd be standing next to Addie Belle onstage, I paired it with a vicious pair of stilettos that put me at well over six feet tall.

Take that, darlin'.

The opening reception was in full swing and seemed to be a great success. The empanadas from a deli in the Bronx were a surprise but were judged to be a charmingly different offering. A number of parents had ponied up a thousand dollars or more to be a part of the reception. Sheree was being gracious about having her picture taken, and Basc Newton could be found in the room by following the ripples of laughter.

And my best friends had arrived. We'd had a glorious reunion. Lovely Cleo looked as lean and beautiful as any ballet dancer (she was an arts and archives expert with the

House of Representatives, but she looked like she could whip off a graceful pirouette on command), and feisty Rita, a whippet next to Cleo's greyhound, was dressed in a conservative blouse and simple skirt—clothes that would never be called slutty. They'd both done me proud.

On her way through DC, Rita hadn't just stopped to pick up Cleo. They'd brought Mimi, too, as a surprise to me. Just seeing the twinkling eyes of my grandmother-by-choice gave me courage and heart and hope.

"Sweetheart!" Mimi cried as she reached up to kiss my cheek. "I'm so proud of you! Look at all these people! What a crowded party!"

"I shook Basc Newton's hand." Rita grinned. "He's cute, huh?"

"Down, girl." I laughed.

"Your dress is perfect," Cleo murmured to me. "You look like a beautiful queen."

"One who might pull out a switchblade, so watch out!" Rita was laughing, and Mimi nudged her.

"Any man who let this treasure go is a fool, don't you think?" she said.

It had taken me a few days to work up the courage to tell my chosen family about Bart and Addie Belle, but when I did, they'd been ready to launch a castration party in my honor. Their support meant everything to me. We didn't have much time to chat at the pre-talent show party, but having all three of them here gave me strength.

I inhaled. It was time.

"I'll be back in a bit. Have an empanada. Panda made them and they're perfect!" I kissed all three of them and moved off. Even though, as the head of the talent show, I needed to be everywhere at once, I took five minutes for myself to cross an item off my to-do list that I was deeply looking forward to.

"Lawrence, I'm sorry to interrupt. Can I pull you away for a moment?"

My boss, stunning in a custom-made suit, was glad-handing a cluster of other masters of the universe (Hamilton Academy definitely had its share), but he looked at me and outright leered. "In that dress? You bet you can, Miss Callie."

I kept my smile in place while mentally kneeing him in the balls. Where was that switchblade when I needed it?

I drew him out of the reception area and into a back hallway. His smile was a little too knowing for his own good.

"You must be doing well in the fundraising department," he said.

"With sponsorships and the pre-party, we're already up to $238,350," I replied.

"A good start before the show even starts. And your work on the AresCorp case has been extremely impressive. Are you anticipating our little talk?"

He'd backed me against the wall and arched into me so I could feel a bulge against my hip. I put my hand on his chest.

"This *is* our little talk, Lawrence. I'm hereby tendering my resignation."

He pulled back, a slow grin warring with a look of suspicion. "Are you joking? You must be joking."

"Not a joke. Here's my letter. I've emailed a copy to the partners." I pulled the page off the clipboard I was holding.

"You don't want to leave now. You won't ever get another job in corporate law."

"I'm not going into corporate law. I'm going into human rights."

I told him I'd been hired by Human Rights Watch. My

salary was a fraction of what I could make with Hoare Ascutney in the future, but it wasn't that much less than I was making now.

Further, I told him his wife had pictures that implied I'd compromised Judge Naughton's impartiality—therefore, either I quit or the judge would need to recuse himself. My resignation was the best option for the firm. Lawrence was left gap jawed.

"Addie did—I'm sorry, what?"

"You might want to speak with her. She said some things that implied she'd done violence to other women you were interested in."

"My god—Helen's accident—"

"I have no specifics. You should look into it. Or not. I don't care either way. Now, I won't be on the AresCorp case on the other side. When I reported all of this to Judge Naughton, he approved my resignation and asked that I not be of counsel in the prosecution of the mercenaries. I agreed, of course. But I'll be working with them on similar cases, and I'm sure we'll meet again—in a court of law. And I'll be learning from the best from now on."

I backed him into the wall and leaned in, not quite touching his chest with a pointing finger.

"AresCorp is going down, and the United States is going to have to take responsibility for the mercenaries they hire. You're going to lose, Lawrence. Enjoy the evening."

Now that was a power exit line. I swept away on a righteous cloud of justice.

What was next on my to-do list?

Alas, the next one wasn't as much fun.

I found him backstage moments before the talent show began. Of course, he had a guitar in hand and was talking with Bump and the band they'd cobbled together. "Bart, can

I talk to you?" He was dressed in a black suit and a blindingly white shirt; his Hamilton Academy school tie set off the blue in his eyes. "Can I have him, Bump? I won't be long."

Bump nodded cautiously. I pulled Bart behind the drop for the opening act.

"I have a speech memorized, and I need to get through it. Can I speak my piece?"

He nodded. "Sure. Are you talking to me now?"

I winced. "I'm apologizing to you. I held you to an impossible standard and blamed you for the actions of others. You and I weren't together when you were with Addie Belle, and I had no right to judge you so harshly."

"Hey," Bump called.

"You've treated Leigh with respect and kindness and you were . . . amazing to me. I've behaved so badly, and I regret so much."

"Hey," Bump said. "We're starting. Sorry, Callie. I get him now."

He dragged his guitarist away, Bart and I both frowning. He hadn't said a word. I felt like I was falling without knowing where I would land.

Leigh raced up. "I've been looking for you! Come on, Addie Belle is talking! You're up next!"

I looked back to Bart—he was looking at me—and then I was thrust out on the stage.

"Here she is!" Addie Belle said brightly. She was wearing a severe red Chinese cheongsam, slit to the hip with a high mandarin collar. She was now ice blonde, with a black Hermès scarf tied in a soft bow at her wrist. "Callie has been a master at running the talent show this year. As you see, we're at the lovely Norbert Theater because the school's auditorium couldn't accommodate all the people who want to enjoy these acts. And we're live online right now, for those who couldn't get tickets! Callie, darlin', won't you tell us all about the donations?"

She turned to me with such a charming smile, I knew she thought I'd have stage fright. But I'd faced down far sterner juries before and had never minded holding the microphone.

"Thank you, Addie Belle. Isn't she wonderful? She does so much for our school. Can we give her a hand?"

I was now holding the mic and she was left with nothing to hold. The applause rolled forth, and she looked perplexed. How had she lost the power in this situation? I went on smoothly, slightly turning my back to her so she felt excluded.

"Tonight, we're raising money for an exciting program—the Hamilton PrimaryNet, a plan to link elementary schools across the state with weather stations that will report to NOAA. It's a great way for students to see the values of science, technology, engineering, and mathematics in action. The first PrimaryNet has been at Hamilton for two years. Now it's time to bring other schools into the net."

Parents in the audience were smiling; they knew of PrimaryNet. Others, lured in by our headliners, weren't so in the know, but interest hadn't yet waned.

"There are nine schools across the state that have applied to be part of PrimaryNet, and they've sent their representatives here tonight."

The spotlight swung up to the stage-left balconies. Grinning children and their parents waved to the audience, who cheered to see them.

"Each station will cost Hamilton Academy $200,000 over three years. That pays for computers, servers, meteorological equipment and installation, and training sessions for teachers and students. And the kids will do all the analysis of the gathered data, overseen by their local TV weathermen as advisers."

The spotlight remained on the adorable faces, so the audience could see the kids who needed their support.

"Now, when you came in, we asked you to register your phones with our volunteers. You'll be able to donate right from your seat. Anyone watching online can donate through the website at the bottom of your screen. And we're looking to everyone for a donation. Any amount will help. We hope we can count on you." I walked over to the large board we'd put up at the side of the stage. "This board shows how many people are watching online, and it will list the total dollars donated during the show. If you gave us permission when you registered, we'll list your name on this board if you donate over $10,000, so others can be inspired by your leadership."

Time to dangle the carrot.

"I'm happy to report that because of corporate sponsorships, ticket sales, and the opening reception, we've already raised $238,350." The total flashed on the board. "And that means . . ."

I turned and pointed to the balcony, where the first school's team screamed with happiness when a white banner unfurled in front of them with the PrimaryNet logo on it.

"Poughkeepsie Elementary 14 will be in the PrimaryNet! I know your school is watching in Poughkeepsie—congratulations. A lot of people have donated to give your school's children a chance at a remarkable STEM program!"

Yes, we were a proud audience. We applauded happily as the winning team cheered and the next few teams in the lineup looked on enviously.

All the way to the end of the stage was my perch. "This is where I'll be sitting, monitoring your generosity. We're having a competition too. I'll be tabulating the donations, and the act that inspires the greatest gift total will win the prize."

"What's the prize?" some determined daddy shouted from the audience.

"King or Queen of the Hamilton Academy Talent Show, of course. What could be better?"

We hadn't been able to agree on a prize that would honor all of our subsets—parent, student, or teacher—so we'd gone with fame and glory instead. It went over well among the acts, and the audience applauded too.

"Now, I had a chat with the managers of our two most famous acts, Basc Newton and Sheree." Just mentioning the names sent up shrieks of joy from the balcony. "They both said separately they'd take themselves out of the running for the competition. Since we're broadcasting live and they both have a lot of fans, they thought it wouldn't be fair. But I told them . . ." I stopped and regarded our audience with a knowing smile. "Our parents love their teachers and know their children can do no wrong, so don't be so sure the pros will walk off with the crown!"

Shouts and screams of approval met this statement. I knew they were as primed to give as I could make them.

"As you can see, there are over six hundred viewers watching online, and I want to welcome them too. This is one performance where you'll be encouraged to use your phones—and your cameras! Fingers on the buttons, Hamilton Academy. Let's get going!"

Addie Belle was caught unawares and had to scurry from the stage when the lights dropped and a spotlight aimed past her to point to our first performer, a mommy who was surprisingly good at baton twirling. The audience shouted with glee.

We were off.

My donation monitor was lighting up already, and I was kept busy updating the big board. Act after act rolled by and the gifts kept coming. Most were small—ten, fifteen, twenty dollars. But occasionally, a three-figure donation would appear, and four-figure gifts weren't unheard of. The number watching through the website was larger than I expected and was slowly trickling upward. We were nearing seven hundred viewers. I attributed this to the Sheree fans who wanted to experience her performance.

We saved our headliners for the second act, figuring the amateurs would have a hard time following Basc Newton or certainly Sheree. By the time we were ready to close out the first act, we'd earned another $243,550. Now two schools had a white banner in front of them. The PrimaryNet had another location.

Then we closed the first act with Leigh's video.

The theater went dark briefly as the large screen was silently lowered. Then Leigh's face appeared.

"I'm Leigh Peacham. I'm in seventh grade at Hamilton. This is my video. Thanks for watching."

The first shot of the video was the third-grade classroom at Hamilton. Phillip McCrillis, Addie Belle and Lawrence's handsome boy, was in the center of the cheerful, carpeted play circle, surrounded by large, brightly colored cushions and his laughing classmates. He was grinning, and the audience applauded their own happily.

Leigh's voice spoke. "What are you doing, Phillip?"

The boy reached out, showing his tablet. "Look. We're looking at the PrimaryNet. See? This line means it's going to snow. See how the dew point is changing? Look right here."

The boy looked up engagingly at the camera and grinned, one missing tooth giving him an adorable look. "I think maybe a snow day tomorrow!"

I heard Addie Belle coo delightedly. The audience cooed along with her.

Then the scene shifted. Now the view was of a cinder-block wall in a classroom painted industrial cream. In rigid steel desks, children kicked their legs and watched the camera with glazed interest. The camera focused on a small face I knew well.

Leigh's voice spoke. "What are you doing, Fonse?"

Fonse was bent over a newspaper, tracing the weather map printed on its page. "Look. See these isobars? With the falling pressure, that means poor weather is heading this way. We might get snow. I don't think so, though. I think there's not enough moisture in the air. The dew point is too high." He looked up. "This is at least twelve hours old, though. Maybe more. So, who knows?"

Leigh appeared again, this time in the main lobby of Hamilton. "That was Alfonso Cabrera. Fonse is in third grade at PS 204 in the Bronx. He's smarter than most of the people you've ever met. Fonse talked his teachers into applying to be part of the Hamilton PrimaryNet. He loves the weather station we have and wishes he could be part of our work with NOAA."

The camera now looked through the pass-through at the Morris Heights Deli, showing Pandora at the grill.

"This is Fonse's mother, Pandora. She makes the best brioche ever in the world. She doesn't know if she wants Fonse to get his hopes up about PrimaryNet. She thinks he's reaching too far."

Pandora's face appeared in an interview-style shot. "Things like that don't happen in the Bronx. I don't want my boy to get his hopes up. We're not rich. It's hard enough on him without being disappointed. I think it's better if the school doesn't apply. Don't you?"

The last shot was of Leigh in the Hamilton front lobby again. "PS 204 in the Bronx was the last school to apply to be a part of PrimaryNet. We'd have to raise $1.8 million at the talent show to get them in. Last year, we raised $1 million, and a lot of people say we can't make more than that. I don't know. But I think Fonse's school deserves a weather station too. If you donate now, maybe they'll get it. Thank you."

The screen went black, and the lights went out. Before the house lights came up, the thunderous applause made me jump in my seat.

They were freaking out. My donation monitor was burning up between the online and in-audience gifts. I hoped we wouldn't fry the server.

The spotlight flipped to the balconies again, and this time, instead of lingering on the winners nearest the stage, it tracked along the row until it came to the last school. Young Fonse was standing up, screaming and waving for all he was worth.

The audience went nuts.

Addie Belle was trying to tell everyone there was a twenty-minute intermission, but a powerful-looking man near the front began calling for her to show the video again. It became a chant that went through the entire theater.

"Again! Again! Again!"

Bowing to the inevitable, Addie waved grandly to the sound booth in the back and moved offstage as Leigh's video played again. As it began, the donations slowed—and then I saw it.

Someone named Anonymous had made a $100,000 donation.

Holy crap.

The video ended and the lights came up. Instead of moving to the lobby for the intermission, the audience turned as one and watched the big board. My hand shook as I typed the total.

Leigh's video had brought in more than $300,000.

The audience was screaming and high-fiving. Online viewership was up over a thousand watchers. Donations went through a second spurt. Leigh's total grew to $324,615.

Two more banners unfurled. Two more schools were in PrimaryNet. Before intermission.

I had to take a few deep breaths to calm down, and then I went backstage to see if I could get my arms around my daughter. I'd barely made it past the first line of curtains when Addie Belle buttonholed me.

20

SECOND ACT

CALLIE

Addie Belle grabbed my arm above the elbow in a pinch tight enough to make me wince. Her usually sweet smile was a frozen rictus as she dragged me deeper into the backstage caverns. When we got to a lonely spot, she swiveled to me, piercing me with her stare.

"What the fuck do you mean, you're quitting?"

Ah. She'd been talking to Lawrence. She was spitting in her fury.

"I'm quitting," I said simply.

"The hell you are. Lawrence needs to win that case. It's worth millions to the firm. You're not leaving, or I'll have you blacklisted." She shook her phone at me menacingly.

"No, you won't. I've already talked to Judge Naughton. He will testify to my innocence. There won't even be a disbarment hearing."

"You talked to—you told him—"

"He knows what you did. He seems to be a pretty discreet man, so news might not travel about your actions. They *might* not."

"You can't prove a thing."

"You're right. I can't. Neither can you."

A look of low cunning transformed her. "But I can still brand your daughter as a discipline case. Or—what about a sexual predator charge for the bio teacher? That's the sort of thing that can ruin a life. You willing to risk that, missy?"

"You're going to leave us alone, Addie Belle. You're not coming near any of us. Here's why."

I tugged the final page off my clipboard and thrust it at her. She took it and tried to make sense of what she was seeing.

"That's your prenup, Addie Belle. You'll see the passage I've highlighted. It says if you have an affair, you don't get a penny from Lawrence."

Addie Belle was blank, looking at the piece of paper with growing horror. Once, she had kicked me when I was down. I made sure to return the favor.

"I'm in a position to prove you've violated your prenup." I nodded across the empty stage to where Bart and Bump had their heads together over some music.

Addie Belle followed my gaze and literally staggered in her heels.

"Is there any possibility that you don't completely understand me, Addie Belle?"

"You bitch!"

"Sweetheart, it takes one to know one. Get away from me."

She tried to gather her dignity but almost immediately got tangled up in a row of curtains she had to fight her way out of.

"Toodles," I said to her fleeing figure.

The stage manager's voice came over the backstage loudspeaker. "Two minutes. We're back in two minutes. Places, please."

No time to find Leigh. No time to see if Bart would forgive me. I went back to my perch at the side of the stage.

We'd crept up to over $815,000 while I wasn't watching. Addie Belle was physically shoved onto the stage by some unseen assistant to introduce the next act. She was shaking and unable to fix her smile properly.

It was time for our two smaller professional acts (the violinist and the dance troupe), and the website audience grew. Those acts were followed by the darling video of the fifth grade's art projects on the theme of friendship. We must have had a lot of fifth-grade parents in the audience, because we were at $863,000 and more than two thousand online watchers by the time Basc Newton took the stage.

He told me later that he was inspired by all he'd seen. The ten minutes on his son's time at Hamilton turned into an impassioned plea for support—and the man was gifted. Funny and touching and colorful. I'd give him his own talk show in a minute. He talked the audience out of another $70,000.

When he finished, I told the crowd that over three thousand people were watching online, and we were within $67,000 of the next school's entry into PrimaryNet. The team from a small private school in the Finger Lakes was clutching each other and screaming. And Lawrence McCrillis, grandstander extraordinaire, stood up on the spot and pledged $128,000, calling out that this was not only enough to fund the school but would push us over last year's total by a thousand dollars.

He'd bailed me out. I couldn't believe it. I'd told him I would snatch his legal victory from him, and he'd helped me beat last year's total.

I looked at him in astonishment as the audience shrieked with excitement and anyone nearby reached out to pat his back or shake his hand.

He looked from me to Addie, shrunken and pale at his side, and nodded to me.

His apology.

I nodded back.

There was a stir onstage, and the school principal stepped forward. He wasn't supposed to speak until before the school song at the end, but I gestured to the sound technicians to go with it.

"Ladies and gentlemen, I've just convened an emergency meeting of the Hamilton Board of Directors here in the lobby. We held an impromptu student-and-family interview, and I'm proud to tell you we have voted unanimously to create a partnership with PS 204 in the Bronx to share teachers, students, ideas, and resources. Our first student ambassador to Hamilton Academy will be PS 204's young Fonse Cabrera."

I couldn't help it. My laughter rippled out of me, along with a few tears.

Fonse was ushered down from the balcony and pushed gently forward, along with Pandora and a handsome Latino man. They were brought to the stage on waves of excitement, and Bump came out from his drum set to hug Panda and pick up Fonse.

"Fonse, we're setting up a two-week summer program at Hamilton to teach members of PrimaryNet how to train their fellow students at home. Whether or not we raise enough tonight to include PS 204 in PrimaryNet, we're inviting you to be a participant—and we've got our eye on you!"

The principal asked Fonse to introduce his family. The

man I didn't know was Uncle Francisco. I remembered Bump had described him as the "hell of a nice guy" gang leader. Francisco caught my eye and waved, his cell phone in his hand.

I suddenly knew who had anonymously donated $100,000. I offered him a respectful bow, which he returned.

The principal looked at the crowd with a smile. "That doesn't mean PS 204 doesn't deserve to be a part of Primary-Net. Can we raise enough to get them in the system?" If applause were dollars, we could. He looked at the cameras broadcasting us onto the web and smiled. "America, will you help?"

I could see our donation amounts were holding steady, and our web audience was growing dramatically as people wanted to see our headliner.

The principal looked around for Addie Belle to introduce the next act. She was nowhere to be found. He shrugged and simply said, "And now, ladies and gentlemen . . . Sheree."

He took Fonse and his family with him when he left the stage, and the fans in the audience shrieked in frantic excitement. Sheree had five Top 10 hits off her current album with two more climbing, and I wasn't sure how many from previous albums. She was one of the hottest singers in the country at the moment, and this was by far the most intimate venue she would play this year. We knew how lucky we were to be there with her. There were now seventeen thousand viewers online.

She opened with a song so omnipresent in this nation that everyone was singing along, from the toddlers in the audience to the grannies. Incredibly, the donations kept pouring in, and the total crept higher and higher.

And she was dazzling. It was easy to see why she was

perpetually waving new Grammy Awards at the cameras that so loved her. She held us all in her hands—and very capable hands they were too.

Between her first and second songs, another school was awarded the PrimaryNet station; that was the sixth. The seventh came after her second, and I realized enough people were broadcasting her concert via their phones, in addition to our school's web presence, that we were now getting small donations primarily from people who were not physically in the building. Of course, the cameras in the audience broadcasting to their friends didn't have the same donation website at the bottom of every shot. Whoever had had the idea to also put the website for donations on the backdrop behind Sheree was a genius.

Oh yeah. That was me.

When the applause died down after Sheree's second hit, she lowered her voice and effortlessly drew the audience into an intimate mood, just the two of them. No one else was around—just every audience member and their absolute best friend, Sheree.

"I have a lot of hits and I love that, but sometimes I come across new music that makes my toes curl. And I have to share it. Want to hear my new favorite song?"

Oh, how we wanted to hear it. She smiled as if she was sharing her deepest secret with only her closest friends and nodded to the band.

Then I heard Bart's guitar. It was the introduction to "Untethered"

She sang the fuck out of that song.

I was sitting at the edge of the stage, sobbing like a baby, but it didn't matter because everyone else was too. The donations stopped, probably because we were all too busy wiping away tears to work our phones. Bart's sorrow became a universal sorrow. Everyone could feel the loss and know it was their own loss and regret pouring forth. He gave us permission to grieve, and we were cleansed by it.

It was a lot to ask of a song, but between them, Sheree and Bart accomplished it.

The audience raised the roof with their applause. Our school server locked out new watchers once we hit twenty thousand viewers, but the donations kept rolling in. The eighth banner rolled down as we crossed over $1.6 million donated. Once more, the powerful man in the front started the "Again!" chant, but Sheree was far more skilled at crowd management than Addie Belle was. She raised her hand for silence, and obediently, we fell quiet.

"You'll hear it again. I'm working on getting permission to record it. Do you know who wrote that gorgeous song?" She offered her million-megawatt grin and walked back to the band, drawing Bart out. "Anyone know this guy? Is this a Hamilton science teacher?"

There were gasps from the audience, and then the applause began again. My hands were hurting, and I looked down to discover I was clapping like mad.

"Ladies and gentlemen, Barton Thetford!"

She gave him a sweet hug around his guitar and backed offstage as he stepped forward.

He was bashful at first, looking down and hiding behind a fall of sandy hair—and then he straightened and waited for the applause to die down. He had a microphone to add backup vocals to the people who sang, so the sound engineer flipped his mic to full power, and he spoke easily.

"I'm glad you liked 'Untethered,' and I'm so excited that Sheree wants to record it. You can't imagine the thrill."

He was interrupted with more applause. We *could* imagine the thrill, and we were proud to share it with him.

"I'm supposed to lead us in the school song now, as the end of the program." The audience emitted a collective *no* of disappointment, and his irresistible grin broke out. "Unfortunately, I'm not done yet, and it helps to be friends with the band."

He grinned at Bump and his musician friends, and the audience laughed in delight.

"I have another song I'd like to debut tonight, if you all don't mind."

We didn't mind. We really didn't mind.

"Thank you. This song is called 'Three.'"

The band launched a groove that made you want to slow dance with someone special. It was a measured rhythm with power behind it. I couldn't explain why, but it had an unexpected wildness to it. Bart began to sing, his voice holding the same power and charisma the audience had grown used to with Sheree.

One was my sister, who chewed all my toys
She sang off-key, made a hell of a noise
She loved the farm, which unlocked my world
She told me one day I'd find a great girl
I loved her, I miss her, I cry at her grave,
My Alison

Three, three, three is the magic number

One is my mother, who dried off my tears,
Made me her flapjacks and called us her dears
Lived for the land that her forefathers tended,
Feels a loss for my sister that cannot be mended
I love her, I miss her, I wish she'd forgive me,
My Samantha

Three, three, three is the magic number

Three women shaped me,
Or hadn't you heard?
I screwed up with two
I won't lose the third

One holds my heart, she's all sass, brass and class
Doesn't mind my crazy, thinks I have a nice butt
Don't call her a muse, - says, "That would
upset me"
I'd slay her dragons if only she'd let me
I love her, I need her, how can I tell her?
My Callie

Three, three, three is the magic number

He was leaving his heart on the stage, opening his soul for the world to examine, and the world welcomed him with a wash of love. His song was a hit before he got to the second verse. They began to sing the chorus with him and loved the joke in the third verse about his ass. He held them in the palm of his hand and found absolution there.

I was a crying wreck. I'd taken to wiping my tears on the hem of my silk dress; there was no alternative. And once he sang my name, half the audience rounded on me, pointing their "live broadcasting" cameras to see my reaction. My reaction was to bury my face on my knees and sob.

When the applause died down, someone called out, "Callie, what's the donation total?"

Christ. Like I could focus after that. A long hand appeared from the well—tall Cleo was handing me a tissue, smaller Rita and Mimi jumping excitedly at her side. My dear friends, supporting me when I needed them. I blotted my eyes and tried to focus.

The answer almost made me sob again. The dollar total was surprisingly low, but no one else had gotten as many donations. Then I saw the names of the donors and realized the pattern.

It was the students who were giving. They were all donating three dollars. Three, in honor of his song.

Three, in honor of the women who had shaped him.

I clicked on my mic and explained why his song had only made $1,821—but as soon as I explained, thousands of other donations pinged in from the audience and from the world beyond, where Sheree's fans were watching our website or some friend-of-a-friend's phone was broadcasting. Some of the donations were for three dollars, some for thirty-three dollars, some for $333. One for $3,000, one for $30,000 (that one, I could see, came from Sheree's manager, obviously at her direction). Before long, his total had climbed to $74,722.

I gulped and logged the total. The crowd cheered.

"I'm proud to say," I said as I rose and tried to smooth my damp skirts, "that the Hamilton Academy has raised $1,974,412 for the PrimaryNet program. PS 204 in the Bronx gets their weather station."

The banner rolled down in front of Fonse's empty seat, and his third-grade teacher, now sitting by herself, screamed and clapped. We screamed and clapped with her.

"I think I can declare a winner of our competition too. Leigh Peacham raised the most money with her video. She is the Queen of the Talent Show."

Leigh appeared from some hidey-hole backstage and took a bow. She brought Fonse with her, and he was a delighted clown for the audience.

"And Mr. Bart Thetford received the greatest number of donations, so let's declare him King of the Talent Show."

Stomping and whistling joined the clapping. Bart stepped forward and bowed grandly over his guitar. Then he bowed to the Queen, and she curtseyed to him. It couldn't have been more perfectly choreographed if we'd been able to preplan it.

When the applause died down, I spoke again. "I think it's time for the school song, and I'm afraid I need a personal minute." They laughed with me and looked to Bart, who was watching me. "We'll keep the donation app open until midnight, but I'm going to shut down the big board. I want to thank you all. So much." I looked to Bart. "Can we have the school song now?"

He grinned. "Not yet."

Christ. I was exhausted.

He looked at Leigh, and she beckoned Olivia and Shane to join her from offstage. They stood in front of him and, because I wasn't already a wreck, they sang the opening lines of "Courage."

At the fork, the gleam of turquoise
To left? To right? What dreams? What joys?
Which chances wait around the bend?
Which path is right? Where waits my friend?

As they sang, other talent show participants slowly filed onstage, singing with them.

There are no wrong choices (Courage)
But you have to make a choice (Courage)
Indecision is the killer (Courage)
Sing out, I need to hear your voice

Courage.

By the time the chorus was over, every child, parent, and teacher who'd participated in the show was onstage, singing. How had he taught them all the song? When had he done it? Why didn't I have even a clue while it was happening?

Your point of view is always changing
From skyscraper heights to water bug's ranging
And all the things you thought you knew
Can vanish in a flash of blue
And all the things you thought you'd seen
Can vanish in a flash of green

For the final chorus, there was a stir as Sheree stepped out again, joining Leigh and Bart at center stage. She opened her million-dollar mouth and out poured the descant I'd heard, weaving in and around all the other voices on the stage. It didn't have the same otherworldly magic I'd heard when Bart and I had sung it alone, but it was still completely breathtaking.

There are no wrong choices (Courage)
But you have to make a choice (Courage)
Indecision is the killer (Courage)
Sing out, I need to hear your voice
Courage.

Okay, I had to admit—that was a finale. As the audience whooped their adoration, I clearly saw Sheree lean over to Bart and I saw her lips form the words, *I want that one too.*

He grinned and quieted the applause by shouting into his mic, "And *now* the school song!"

Bump led them off, and everyone in the place seemed to know the words I had yet to learn. From the mass of people on the stage, Bart caught my eye and gestured with his chin backstage. Abandoning all pretense of formality, I simply stood, walked around the corner, and followed him into the wings.

We met at center stage behind the backdrop. I tried to think of something to say but couldn't. Instead, I held out my hands to show him how red they were from clapping.

He took them reverently and raised them to his lips, kissing each palm, and I thought my heart would stop.

"You forgive me?" I asked, my voice filled with tears.

"Do *you* forgive *me*?"

He was crying, too, so I didn't feel out of place. "Don't be an ass."

"I am an ass." He grinned at me.

"And you have a nice one."

"Nice what, Callie?"

I stepped into his arms. "You have a nice ass, Mr. Thetford. I'm in love with you."

"Damn it! I wanted to say it first!"

"Say it second."

He stopped teasing and looked into my eyes. "I love you, Callie. And not just because you're my muse. I'll try so hard to never disappoint you."

"I know you will. Same goes. Is your nose too clogged to kiss me?"

"Watch and learn, girl."

His arms came around me as if he'd never let me go. I was holding on as tightly, my fingers buried in his hair. The kiss felt like redemption, like the burst of hope. I was melting in his arms.

Dimly, I sensed a change in our environment. Had it suddenly gotten brighter? The school song came to an end at last and wild applause rang out.

We broke from our kiss to find that clever Fonse had figured out how to raise the backdrop, and we were wrapped in an all-encompassing kiss at center stage, surrounded by the school, the audience, some of Hollywood's most celebrated stars, and the gleam of phones in the hands of the few who weren't cheering and clapping for us.

Now, *that's* what I call a finale. Public display of affection? I plead guilty, Your Honor, but with extenuating circumstances. You should have seen his ass.

Author breaking in here while you're all gooshy and happy: If you're reading an ebook, then once you turn this page, Amazon is going to ask if you want to rate this book. Like it, love it, hate it—no matter how you feel, will you please do it? Amazon watches to see which books readers respond to. No matter your rating (five stars is best, hint-hint!), you'll help me train the Amazon algorithm to suggest this book to other readers. Will you? Smooch!

Okay—now time to say....

THE END

WANT TO READ CLEO'S STORY?

History's Muse

"Excuse me," a soft baritone voice said. At the door, a Glorious Son of Our American Midwest was leaning in—tall, built, wheat-blond hair thick on his handsome head. "I'm Joseph, from I.T. I need to upgrade your security window units. Is this a bad time?"

It's no surprise that Cleo is tired. After all, she's been through a lot. Can she be blamed for secretly longing for a 1950s-style traditional relationship? Cleo wishes she could meet a man to love her, care for her, take on all the crisis management. Even though she knows it goes against the code of strong, independent modern women, Cleo is husband-hunting.

When Joseph meets Cleo, he's dazzled. The beautiful manager of the Department of Art and Archives at the U.S. House of Representatives is lovely, quiet, sweet. He would fall in love with her and offer her marriage if only she would convert to his religion.

It seems like a small price to pay for Cleo. She has no

religious beliefs of her own; why not follow her future husband's faith if it makes him happy? But Cleo has to face some searching questions. What is she willing to sacrifice to find her perfect marriage? Is Joseph really the right man for her, or is she overlooking something important right in front of her?

BLISS & GIGGLES

Sign up for my newsletter, sweetpea! Go to https://pruwarren.com

My newsletter philosophy? Never take yourself too seriously. Skip the boring stuff. Amuse yourself; maybe others will be amused too.

There's generally a smoochy gift to thank you for signing up. As of this writing, I'm offering a blissful little novella called JOAN'S JOURNAL for newsletter subscribers, which features your choice of a clean-and-sweet epilogue or a hot-and-spicy version where they go at it like rabbits. Your choice; no judgment.

But I swap up my newsletter lure from time to time. Go see what I'm dangling in front of you today; maybe you'll find it tasty!

ABOUT THE AUTHOR

Pru Warren (who is writing this in the third person as if simply too modest to toot her own horn) bores easily and thus has been a daydreamer since roughly the Bronze Age.

She is addicted to writing because in a novel, you can make things come out the *right* way. Life and karma really ought to take note. There are *better solutions* to these pesky daily annoyances!

Besides her in-the-laptop God complex, Pru laughs often and easily, loathes cooking, and plays way too much solitaire. She's plotting world domination even as you read this, as long as she doesn't have to wake up too early to accomplish it.

The Pru Warren website is an action-packed laff riot. (Well, it ought to be, anyway.) You can explore at https://www.pruwarren.com/

ALSO BY PRU WARREN

The Muse Books

City Muse

History's Muse

Untamed Muse

Cupid's Quest:

Cupid's Quest Season One

Cupid's Quest Season Two

Cupid's Question Season Three

The Ampersand Series:

Cyn & the Peanut Butter Cup

Dash & the Moonglow Mystic

Ellyn & the Would-Be Gigolo

Farrah & the Court-Appointed Boss

The Surprise Heiress Series:

Breath of Fresh Heiress

Full of Hot Heiress

Vanished Into Thin Heiress

You Decide Books:

Emma's Mission

A Spirit Guide for Anna Maria

Joan's Journal (Love Gone Viral) (out of print, alas, but available free in ebook form to newsletter subscribers) (hint, hint)

Made in United States
North Haven, CT
04 November 2023

43602805R10115